About the Author

Nial Giacomelli spent his childhood between England and the US. He attended the University of Portsmouth, studying Media, before becoming a software developer. *The Therapist* is his debut novella.

The Therapist

NIAL GIACOMELLI

Fairlight Books

First published by Fairlight Books 2019

Fairlight Books
Summertown Pavilion, 18-24 Middle Way, Oxford, OX2 7LG

A CIP catalogue record for this book is available from the
British Library

1 2 3 4 5 6 7 8 9 10

ISBN 978-1-912054-90-9

www.fairlightbooks.com

Printed and bound in Great Britain by Clays Ltd

Designed by Sara Wood

Illustrated by Sam Kalda
www.folioart.co.uk

For Tora. For everything.

I

When the anguish between us grows so palpable that it manifests veins and a nervous system, an entire body that darts from beneath bed frames and behind dressers to howl the night away, I finally relent and agree to meet with a therapist. The promise floats round in the dark of my mind until finally it materialises and I find myself alone one afternoon on country roads.

I drive west as a heavy snow begins to fall, leaving the distant murmur of the city for more rural country. I pass sleepy houses with sash windows and steeped dormers, an old asylum with an imposing portico, the vague shapes of evening shoppers among a quaint collection of storefronts, until gradually the houses begin to disappear, replaced instead by a series of abandoned warehouses and outbuildings. They tell a sad history of slow, generational death, their sheet metal falling away, their brickwork slowly crumbling, until they themselves are gone.

When I finally spot the black mass of the therapist's stately home I have all but given up hope. It comes into focus through the early evening light and I feel my apprehension like a stone at the pit of my stomach. The property is alive with Gothic spires and buttresses, a mess of stonework and wooden lattice. It looks like something out of a Shirley Jackson novel and as I pass beneath the cast iron gate and ascend the path beyond I begin to consider the impossibility of my own reality.

From the car I take a moment to inspect the black shingles of the house. There is such a sense of dereliction to the place that I am almost surprised when I notice a woman watching from one of the upstairs windows. She has a shock of white hair and stands so still that I think for a moment she must be a trick of the light.

Simone waits for me beneath the eaves of the house. As I approach she turns to greet me and at the sight of her face I feel a great exhaustion wash over me. The muscles in my legs suddenly weak. The pain so intense that for a moment I fear I won't be able to get out of the car. But when she nods her head and beckons for me to join her I know that she understands. That she is aware of my apprehension, my reservations about the undertaking.

We stand before the house's imposing red door. I lift its metal knocker, a brass lion, and am surprised by the weight of it in my hand. I crane my head upwards, expecting to find a portcullis, some piece of arcane medieval apparatus high above us, but I see only wooden beams.

The therapist escorts us through the property in silence. We are ushered into a room and sit beneath a crude landscape painting of the sea. I watch snow fall through the property's arched windows. It is unending. I imagine it piling up round the house, covering the windows and blocking the doors, rising to the roof and further still to cover the chimney until we disappear completely. I can feel winter's cold hands against the house, resting on window ledges and pressing into doors, trying desperately to work its way inside.

'Shall we get started?' the therapist asks finally and I feel my body tense.

On the carpet a lazy square of sunlight stretches itself across the room in the way a cat might. I use it to keep track of time.

Simone sits, hands folded in her lap, and she weeps.

She cries his name so much it begins to sound foreign.

A broken, useless thing. And it is.

The dead have no use for names.

After the session I throw the journal the therapist has given us onto a heap of snow and sit inside the stifling cold of my car. Simone raps on the driver's side window with her knuckle. When I wind it down she brushes dirt from the cover of the notebook and kneels to look me in the eye.

'We have to at least try,' she says.

'Did you try, Simone?' I ask and regret it immediately.

She stands and though I cannot see her face I know that she is holding back tears. Her body shakes and rattles with the effort. I contemplate getting out of the car and comforting her, but instead find myself putting it in reverse.

I leave her standing alone in the snow, my breath forming clouds as I descend the gravel path. I don't need to look for her in the rear-view mirror to know what I'll see. Head hung, hands clasped over mouth. Face pale, eyes sunken. The same listless and forlorn expression. A ghost.

That night she writhes and thrashes in her sleep, sweat dampening the sheets round her like a halo. She calls out to him and weeps, her hands held high above her as if reaching for some imagined and unreachable landmark.

When she wakes it is morning.

'I dreamt we were at sea,' she says.

II

We are told to use the journals to write stray thoughts and observations between sessions. It's a vague assignment that I find more irritating than liberating. And though I make a few genuine attempts, all I can ever bring myself to write about is how punishingly tired I feel.

'It's as if someone is cutting into me while I sleep and gradually stitching weights into the muscles and tendons of my body. And though it's not debilitating I find it harder each day to fight to the surface. To re-become myself,' I read aloud during our next session.

'And is that what you want?' the therapist asks. 'To re-become yourself?'

I think about that in the dark on the way home, my car illuminated every so often by passing headlights. And when I see the house approaching I consider blowing straight past it. Just disappearing into the night.

When I pull into the driveway Simone is sat on

the doorstep waiting for me. She palms up a fistful of snow and rubs it into her cheeks. When she pulls her hands away her face is shot red with the shock, her skin alive and screaming, and I am almost relieved.

III

There is a newfound levity to Simone in the weeks after we begin therapy. It's as if a cloud has begun to lift. Early one morning I suggest we take a drive into the city and to my surprise she agrees. I can hardly remember the last time she left the house for any kind of recreational pursuit. As I help her into the car I realise I am holding my breath. I allow myself, for the briefest moment, to hope. Perhaps the fresh air will do her good, I think. Perhaps some time away is all she'll need.

She sits with her hands folded in her lap and as I merge onto the freeway I tell myself that we have turned a corner. But with each passing mile I feel a tension building in the car. Her hands reaching up slowly to cross her chest, her muscles bracing for some imagined impact.

We order breakfast at a small diner we used to visit often. Simone had been instantly smitten by the place when we first stumbled upon it. She used to say it made her feel like she was part of an Edward Hopper painting. The chefs here wear paper forage hats and go about their work in immaculate white smocks. They serve comfort foods. Pie with ice cream, coffee and eggs.

We sit in a booth and watch as patrons shuffle in and out of doorways, as they hop on and off bar stools. Behind us a young couple sit hand in hand. They lean into each other and whisper. I watch them and try to imagine their darkest secrets, to fantasise their intimacies. They touch the napes of each other's necks. They giggle.

'We used to come here all the time,' I say. 'Do you remember?'

She nods and smiles faintly, pushing a napkin along the table in ever smaller circles. Somewhere a child laughs and she winces. When the waitress returns with our food I'm glad for the interruption. Simone mushes her food into a fine paste, until it is a slurry, and then she sets it aside.

'I don't think I can eat,' she says, raising her hands up to blot at the corners of her mouth.

This comes as no surprise but it still irritates me. She is never hungry. I cook each night and watch in the dark of the kitchen as she takes little conciliatory bites. She chews the pieces dramatically, chasing them with sips of water, and each night she gives me the same frail smile as if she is expecting a standing ovation, or perhaps my eternal gratitude.

I feel my disappointment rattle through me. I close my eyes and wait for it to radiate out of my body like an aftershock. I try to remind myself that we are both victims. But when I open my eyes I notice she is distracted, staring out of the window at some distant landmark, and my irritation begins to rise up again. My anger burns inside of me, the flames licking at my throat, trying desperately to reach open air. She is sick, I tell myself. She is sick but she makes no attempt to get better.

'It's good,' I say, lifting the food from my plate in great heaps, chewing it with an open mouth to irritate her.

She smiles distractedly and stares off again, this time towards the deli counter, where a small crowd has gathered. They shuffle anxiously as they watch the breaking news. Slowly the murmur of conversation begins to die down, trickling off gradually as people strain their ears to listen to the broadcast.

In Oregon the air is alive with the sound of sirens. The sick are collapsing in the streets, their bodies piling up in clinics and hospitals. The footage looks like a strange fiction.

When someone asks a waitress to change the channel she shrugs.

'It's on every channel,' she says.

Members of the public are urged to contact emergency services if close relatives experience severe headaches, disorientation or a fever that persists for more than two days. Symptoms in the later stages of the illness are said to include a swelling of the face, a reddening of the eyes, auditory and visual hallucinations and a feeling of pronounced euphoria.

Investigators have so far been unable to determine

a means of transmission. It's not airborne, they say. It's not sexually transmitted. 'But it's clearly communicable,' the telecaster says, 'given the sheer number of reports we're receiving.'

Simone wrings her hands. 'What do you make of it?' she asks.

I study the troubling images on the television screen. The vast emergency response, the clear severity of the illness. I take an immediate, if slightly shameful, solace in the fact that we are half a country away. That there are thousands of miles separating us from any perceivable threat.

'A feeling of pronounced euphoria? I think we're going to make it,' I say.

She is silent for a moment and then, forgetting herself, lets out a snicker. It is the first time I've heard her laugh in months. The sound slips out of her, a living thing fleeing a desolate fate. Her eyes widen and she clasps a hand over her mouth. The crowd turns their attention in her direction; some shake their heads.

I take her hand and lead her out of the restaurant. We venture into the cold together and look back at the congregation through the diner window. They gather round the television as if it is a religious artefact, a barer of elemental truths. They stand with their mouths agape, their hands clasped, and I realise then that we have become separated, somehow, from the world at large. That their concerns are no longer our concerns. Their urgency, the volume of their rising fear, has been quieted in us.

IV

It takes the body months to reconcile what the mind knows as truth.

He is gone, but not entirely.

He is remembered, but not completely.

The body struggles with this. There are brief moments of panic. Waves of nausea when we think that we have forgotten to collect him from school. Moments in busy crowds when we think he has disappeared from our side. Mornings when we open his bedroom door and call out his name. There are baths drawn but never occupied. Plates prepared but left untouched. Car doors opened and closed in a single, mournful gesture.

The mind is solemn. Though it grieves, it knows there is little use.

But the heart, the body, is stubborn. Its muscles reach out, its skin yearns.

And so we busy ourselves with the act of survival. We eat and drink. We shovel snow from the driveway and tend to the house. We return to work so that we may pay our bills. But the purpose is diminished. Who are we working for, if not him?

We cannot be alone together.

We cannot even be alone with ourselves, for he is with us now always. His memory is tethered to ours. His life was our life. His death is our death, for we have been forever changed.

We receive cards and flowers, tokens of commiseration. We see friends and co-workers.

We are sorry for your loss, they say.

We forget, almost, that his name was not 'your loss'.

Everyone is sorry, yet no one speaks his name.

V

At night our sorrow lies between us, its weight pulling at the bedsheets in much the same way the boy would when seeking safe haven from bad dreams and thunderstorms.

In the dark I am taken back to the days and weeks that followed his death. I remember the stillness and vacuum-like quiet. The collective holding of breath by those who visited to offer their condolences. Even the house was changed by his passing.

You could hear small creaks and groans as its foundations shifted and settled in the night. If you strained your ears the sound of laughter radiated from behind closed doors. From a certain spot in the living room, when you sat still enough, you could sometimes make out the patter of phantom feet in the hallway.

Simone would wake often in panic and rush to his room, her face sheet-white in the darkness. She swore that she could hear him calling out to her from the darkened corners of the house, from beneath doorframes and down flights of stairs.

I caught her once in the attic, tipping out the contents of boxes, searching desperately for his old baby monitor – weeping when she found it without power, the batteries long dead. She was sure, she said, that she could hear him over the tinny speaker. That he was calling her name.

For months she was sick with the grief. Rendered almost catatonic by a weight that hung heavy in both her mind and body. She refused to eat and spent her days wandering the halls aimlessly, drifting from room to room as if he might suddenly appear from behind the kitchen island or beneath the staircase.

There were only brief reprieves. Moments of stillness that hinted at stability, a chance to return to a sort of normalcy. But they were fragile, disturbed by the simplest of discoveries. A photograph hidden between the pages of a book could send her reeling. A tiny sandal discovered beneath a piece of furniture. An article of clothing that triggered her olfactory memory and brought him back to her for the cruellest of moments.

She suffered stress headaches, much like she had as a teenager, migraines that would blossom like cactus flowers in the depths of her eye sockets. She was struck by a terrible malaise that kept her bedridden. And though I knew only stories of her youth, I was forced to watch helplessly as the wounds of her depression reopened across the geography of her body.

In his absence I directed the excess of my attention towards her. I bathed and fed her, caring as best I could.

On good days she would take small sips of soup, and between mouthfuls I would try to reason with her. I would stroke her hair and beg. But inevitably she would rebuff my attempts, slapping me away to drift upstairs and draw herself a bath.

I would sit on my knees and watch through the keyhole as she stripped naked and submerged herself in the scalding water, her skin turning lobster pink as she opened her eyes and held her breath for as long as she could bear before wrenching upwards and gasping for breath.

'Oh God,' she would howl. 'Oh God.'

VI

At the beginning of each session the therapist steeps a pot of tea, serving the liquid in porcelain cups and saucers that she delivers on a steel tray reminiscent of a piece of surgical equipment, something you might have found in an operating theatre at the turn of the century. It is a strange and disconcerting juxtaposition.

I decline the offer of a beverage but Simone partakes. I can tell that she is fond of the therapist, but in truth I find the woman deeply unsettling. Her eyes are so dark they seem to swallow the light round them; her gaze so intense, so unwavering in its certainty, that I feel myself carried away by it.

I witness her only in fleeting glances, stolen moments. Her look is timeless not in the sense that it evades antiquation, but that it simply cannot be placed. Though her hair is silver her age proves increasingly difficult to determine. She takes a moment to compose herself before speaking, as if the act of cognition weighs heavily, but she moves in a manner that betrays her appearance, suggesting a certain youthfulness.

When I ask whether it's common for a person in her field to work out of their own home she says, 'I am in the business of intimacy. This has been my home for as long as I can remember having one. It was my father's, and his father's before him. It seemed only fitting.'

In the days leading up to our first appointment I imagined the building as part of a vast institute. I saw pretentious men loitering in lab coats. Long hallways with polished floors that smelt faintly of ammonia. Concrete walls in gradations of dull pastel colours. Obscure and vaguely phallic sculptures.

And perhaps that is why the therapist speaks to Simone with a delicate humility but seems to regard me with a certain hostility, a remoteness that borders on condemnation. She considers me a sceptic, a non-believer. I have never experienced the types of depressive fits Simone finds herself prone to. The kind of sadness that falls upon a person like winter snow. Thick and suffocating and entirely without reason.

Though I try to remain sympathetic during our sessions, I find myself repeatedly insisting on actionable change, measurable progress. Instead we talk increasingly about the regalia of loss. We discuss our dreams endlessly. Simone says that she can see him so clearly when she closes her eyes that it hurts. But to me the memory of his face remains indistinct, elusive. Like something from another time.

The therapist listens to Simone intently but thanks me for my contributions in a way that feels like an act of placation, as if I am a child on some rambling, inarticulate monologue. Each time she speaks I feel my frustration like a knot at the centre of my chest. I try to will it away.

I watch as she adjusts the hem of her dress, the rim of her glasses, and feel a simmering heat inside of me. When I look round her office I spot diplomas and accolades, but not a single family photo. I wonder if she even has a family. I wonder if our blight, our sorrow, is even remotely relatable to her, or if this is all just a sad academic exercise.

It upsets me too that while she carries a notepad I never see her make note of anything during our sessions. Is our pain so pedestrian, I wonder? So transient as to not even be noteworthy?

'Who does this help?' I ask suddenly, surprising myself, digging my fingers so deeply into my calf that my knuckles turn white. 'Who does this help, this endless repetition?'

'Please don't,' Simone says, resting a hand on my knee.

The gesture takes me by surprise. It feels invasive, but perhaps not altogether unwelcome. It reminds me of a time before all of this, when things were easier. When we had less to forget.

I raise my palms up slowly. 'This feels pointless.'

'Dreams can admittedly seem abstract,' the therapist says, 'but if you take the time to listen to them I think they can have an immensely positive impact. Sleep is ultimately a time for introspection.

A chance for the mind to explore itself. And so much of what and how we dream is controlled by our emotional state. Our surroundings, the realities we deal with each and every day, all of it takes a toll.'

VII

In my dreams my mind walks like a trapeze artist between the topology of my history and my desires for the future. A delicate balance between what is and was, and what now can never be.

Each night I become a younger version of myself. I sit beside Simone in a coffee shop and rub my clammy hands so much it looks like I have a skin condition. I make silly self-deprecating remarks and she assures me that everything is fine. She puts her hand in mine and smiles in a way that makes her eyes shine brighter than I thought possible.

She moves in gradually, the walls of my apartment filling with art deco prints and needlepoint, the hallways teeming with lush ferns and colourful rugs. There are shelves in each room overflowing with various ornaments and trinkets, the spoils of our adventures together. In our bedroom is a noticeboard covered in ticket stubs and photographs. On our windowsill sits a ceramic *maneki-neko*, a lucky cat that neither of us can remember buying.

At some indiscernible point the apartment ceases to be mine and instead becomes ours. Her contentment seeps its way into the fabric of throw cushions and bedsheets. Her perfume settles on clothes and lingers in the air. The very smell of her makes me feel like I am home. She becomes my place in the world.

We marry and save for years before taking a belated honeymoon across Europe. We travel by steam train and ferry, by bus and gondola. We sleep in hotels and hostels and sleeper cars. We read together in coffee shops and slowly we learn the richness of the continent's history.

We walk hand in hand along endless cobbled streets. We visit medieval churches and amphitheatres. We stand at the foot of fjords. We visit vineyards and rustic wood-panelled taverns. We eat on rooftop terraces, beneath rose-covered trellises. By day we explore the geography of the continent and at night we explore the geography of each other. Two shapes that come together as one.

We buy a house and before the last of the boxes are unpacked Simone tells me she is pregnant. Later, she gives birth to a healthy baby boy. We name him Phineas, and at night I sit and listen to him taking tiny breaths in the dark. In the mornings we have whispered arguments over nothing, born from sheer exhaustion.

We make a home for the child and the child grows to fill it. He is six months old, then a year. He is two and can already catch a ball. I shut my eyes for the briefest of moments and when they reopen he has learnt to read and write. He turns five. We throw a large party with streamers and paper hats. He has his mother's compassion, her sense for people. At night we indulge his love of folktales.

Then, one day, he is gone from us and my dreams take the form of impossible realities. I imagine a future where he is still alive. Where years have passed and he is now a teenager. I dream that my hair thins but thankfully doesn't disappear completely. And when Simone survives a cancer scare we celebrate with a return trip to Europe, our angsty son in tow.

We find the peaks harder to climb. The cobbles wreak havoc on our feet. The history seems a little less electric, somehow. A little less alive with possibility. Secretly I feel as though the horizon of my life may have begun to recede.

But in our quieter moments it's as if nothing has changed. We drag Phineas to monument after endless monument. He stands taller each day, the human summation of our love. He exhales loudly when we insist on including him in photographs, and in bars and cafés we notice his attention drawn elsewhere, to girls with accents and tattoos and sundresses.

I watch him and remember the day he took his first steps. I thumb my knuckles and think of all the steps since then. Somehow, I tell myself, I thought I'd have known more by now.

Simone takes my hand and wraps it in hers.

She smiles at me, the light of her face enveloping us both, and I lose track of the boy.

'Phineas?' I call out. 'Where is Phineas?'

When I wake it is morning. The bed is wet with sweat on both sides.

She rolls to face me.

'I dreamt we were at sea,' she says.

VIII

I watch the humanitarian crisis in Oregon unfold through newspaper headlines and televised coverage. There is an unending stream of social media updates and amateur video footage. Slowly I become familiar with the geography of the place. The names of its cities and towns. Its streets and thoroughfares.

I'm introduced to the increasingly tired and dishevelled congregation that represents its local government. They stand behind makeshift podiums in municipal buildings and school gymnasiums. They rub the bridges of their noses and shift on the balls of their feet outside medical centres and firehouses.

The illness spreads quickly, entrenching itself. It becomes increasingly clear that the authorities are fighting a war of attrition. Through daily press conferences I watch their professional demeanour unravel much like their attire: ties loosen, buttons come undone, shirts untuck.

Under the blinding light of the cameras I watch as the situation slowly takes its toll on their bodies.

I see their stooped shoulders, their waxy skin, the vacancy in their eyes. I begin to refer to them on a first-name basis. Slowly a kinship develops, a compassionate allowance. Like a distant relative, I fret over their well-being.

The national papers run with a full-page photograph showing a young doctor weeping against the façade of a hospital. I find myself fascinated by it. There is an undeniable gravity to the photo. A sense of history in its making. Who is this woman, I wonder, this unattributed soul?

Her eyes are ringed and sunken, her skin puffy. She is crouched low to the ground as if she expects it to shift beneath her, but in truth I believe it already has. I imagine that she has not been home in days. That she has paged chief residents, fellows, attending physicians, department heads. That her questions remain unanswered. The nature of the illness, the things she has witnessed, have invalidated the axioms of her own understanding. The bedrock of her reality has shifted.

I know this because I have lived through a similar crisis of understanding. I stood months earlier beneath the punishing fluorescent lights of a hospital wing while a doctor explained that our son was gone. I watched as Simone shut down, failing entirely to process the news.

'Thank you,' she said after the doctor was finished. 'May we please speak with him now? He must be terrified.'

Much like his birth, the reality of his death hit her in waves of pain. He was gone, and by extension so too was a piece of her. And perhaps that is why I find the photograph so captivating. There is a candour to it. It captures the immediate aftermath of loss. It is an overtly human moment.

I sit cross-legged in front of the television until late afternoon. I watch as authorities race to establish cordons in an attempt to slow the spread of the illness, as they erect tents to filter the incoming sick. Like footage of the Great Depression there are lines of people stooped and coughing. Corridors full of gurneys. Ambulances circled like wagons, their flashing lights illuminating the falling snow round them.

They play footage of loved ones being escorted to and from hospitals. Siblings and parents, grand-mothers and uncles. Some weep openly, others hold handkerchiefs to their mouths, the rest walk with a grim determination. No one stops to speak with the press. When I try to discuss the case with Simone she begs me to turn it off. She can't even bear to hear about it.

Though the media blackout is fairly effective, a local network is able to secure an interview with an off-duty nurse. She talks into the camera from a dimly lit hotel room, her features distorted, blurred in a way that makes her face look like a blank sheet of flesh. No eyes or mouth. And when she speaks I hear only a distant tinkling sound, like glass scraping glass.

'They fall into a sort of waking sleep,' she says.

But there are moments of consciousness. Frantic whispers.

'It took us a while to realise that they were talking about each other,' she says.

That they were recalling memories, but not their own. Never their own.

They were speaking of things they couldn't possibly know.

Things before them.

Things beyond them.

IX

It snows all through the night. Before I even finish shovelling the driveway there is a fresh flurry settling. I walk into the street and look it up and down. There are low skies and barren trees for as far as the eye can see. Nothing moving in either direction, the snow undisturbed.

I turn back and study the house. It sits set back slightly from the road, the front yard bordered by a series of dwarf hedges. My eyes run along its gabled roof and then down to the broken pediment that sits over the large, panelled front door. I try to assess it objectively, to determine whether I would still be interested as a potential buyer. It is one of the smaller properties on the block, but it is by no means a small property.

We'd bought it the year Simone became pregnant, when the world still felt imbued with magic. It was the first property either of us had ever owned. And it was difficult now, six years on, to imagine having lived anywhere else. There were places before, of course.

Various apartments: hers and mine, then mine *with her*, and finally *ours*. But those places seem to have crystallised in my mind. Though they still exist it's hard to imagine us ever having occupied them. Through the haze of memory I seem to have reduced each to a list of unfortunate deficiencies: noisy neighbours, leaky faucets, broken stovetops.

Simone had always hated the congestion of the city. She wanted to raise a family in the kind of place she had grown up. Where neighbours knew each other's names, and people looked out for one another. But I'd been incredibly reluctant about leaving the city. I had spent my entire life there. It felt like an intrinsic part of me, a piece of my identity. There was a certain sense of anonymity to metropolitan life that I found appealing. Where Simone felt diminished by gathering crowds, I felt a sense of empowerment.

In the end we compromised and bought a family home in a quiet suburb on the outskirts of Chicago. It was the kind of place my parents used to drive past and wished desperately to call their own.

I would joke that I could still see the taillights of the moving van when Simone announced her pregnancy. She would slap my hand when I mentioned the suspicious timing at dinner parties and insist that I was being outrageous, but we both knew there was an element of truth to it.

I'd been unpacking boxes in the master bedroom when she picked up a magazine and began reading it aloud. Moving was the third most stressful life event you could experience, it said, after the death of a loved one and the loss of a job.

She'd lost her mother six months earlier, a sudden illness that had shocked us both in its cruelty, and she'd chosen to leave her work in the city to focus on the move, on our new life in the suburbs.

'Are we crazy for doing this?' she asked.

I took her hand and kissed it, turning the pale skin over and running my fingers along the faint veins of her arm.

'This is what you wanted. This is what we both wanted.'

'And it's wonderful,' she said, 'but it's so much, so fast.'

I could see the worry on her face. She wore it like a veil.

'What are we really talking about here?' I asked.

She lifted the magazine and pointed to the fourth life event: pregnancy.

'Let's hold fire on that one.'

But she took my hand and placed it on her belly. 'That ship may have already sailed.'

'You've done a test?' I asked, but I already knew the answer. I knew her. I knew that if I went to the study and opened her laptop I'd find exhaustive searches for the best brands available. That she would have snuck out early to purchase them, interrogating the pharmacist before returning home to confirm her suspicions in private.

'Can I see it?' I asked.

We went into the en-suite and she handed me the little piece of plastic. I sat on the lip of the bathtub and stared at it in silence.

'You're pregnant?' I said, almost incredulous. She stood in the doorway and nodded slowly, her eyes welling with tears. 'You're pregnant,' I said again, and then I rose and hugged her. I kissed the skin of her neck and we held each other in silence.

'You're pregnant!' I roared, lifting her up and forcing a giggle out of her.

That night we walked together beneath the stars, which, like the child, seemed so unnervingly close and yet so impossibly beautiful. And with each footfall the enormity of the obligation seemed to dawn on me.

Beneath the milk white of the moon I thought back to my own childhood. To my parents' arguments over mortgage payments and tuition, schedules and social functions. To my father, who had taken on the form of a poltergeist in our young lives, leaving early for work and appearing late at night to upset furniture and dishes while we slept. To the din of worry that seemed to play out so unrelentingly.

And later, beneath the sheets, with the boxes piled all round us, I had relayed all of my fears to her. I had left them naked and bare at her doorstep like an infant. And she had chased each of them away in turn.

I felt then as though I would be happy to remain with her forever. Her legs swimming beneath the sheets, intertwined with mine. The warmth radiating off her.

But it's difficult now, all of these years later, not to appreciate the bitter irony of our situation. We had built a life around the child, but now the child was gone. Like the apartments we once inhabited the thought of life before him feels alien, like a memory borrowed from a stranger. He is woven into the fabric of our shared existence that his death has rendered our life counterfeit. Without him, I wonder, what remains of us? Of our life together?

X

Every few months I open the en-suite's mirror cabinet and inventory the medicines we keep there. The collection seems to grow each year. There had been a time when all I seemed to need was antiperspirant and toothpaste. Now the cabinet overflows with eczema creams and nasal sprays. There are heat packs and muscle balms stacked in uneven piles, all manner of decongestants and heartburn tablets. A litany of migraine medications.

On the lowest shelf are Phineas's old medicines. Bottles of dinosaur-shaped vitamins, plastic syringes, liquid paracetamol, tubes of antiseptic ointments. I lift each and quietly drop them into the trash can at my feet. The act feels illicit, a subtle betrayal, and I go about my work quietly, praying that Simone won't hear me.

At the back of the cabinet, hidden in a floral bag, I find a pill bottle. I pick it up and turn it over in my hand. Simone's initials are printed across the label and beneath it, in block capitals, is the name of a drug I don't recognise. When I type it into my phone the results suggest they are a sleep aid, but in all the time

I've known her she's never struggled with insomnia.

When I hear her stirring in the bedroom I return the bottle to its hiding place and turn off the lights. I stare at her from the doorway. I consider mentioning the discovery but decide against it.

'You're still reading that?' I ask as I lift the covers and slide in beside her.

She turns the book over in her hand and studies the cover. 'I can't seem to finish it. I read a page but nothing sticks. I try to focus on a paragraph. A sentence. But I can't make any progress.'

'Why not start something new?'

'It would feel too much like breaking a promise,' she says.

When I look at her face it seems wrong, somehow, as if the discovery of the pill bottle has altered my perception of her. I turn my bedside lamp off and watch as she does the same. We lie together in the darkness. I think about the pills. How long had she been taking them? Why would she feel the need to hide them?

I find myself unusually conscious of her presence, as if I am sleeping next to a stranger. I feel the heat of her body but it brings me little comfort. There had been a time when I considered us fundamentally the same person, but lately I feel a chasm opening between us. I consider for a moment the disquieting notion that a life need not be actively abandoned or dismantled, but simply observed with growing distance until one day it is no longer your own.

'Do you remember the week we brought him home?' she asks suddenly.

She rolls to face me and I can see her eyes in the darkness. They reflect a light that doesn't exist. The flickering embers of a campfire in some imagined distance.

'I remember.'

'The only place you could get him to settle was here, between us.'

'You were worried because all the books said it was dangerous.'

'When he finally fell asleep I asked you if you loved him. Do you remember what you said?'

'I do.'

There is a silence between us. A longing. I feel her body tense as she speaks the words. 'Tell me again.'

I sigh, suddenly exhausted. 'Simone.'

'Please. Just once.'

'I said that I did. But that it was a new sort of love. A desperate, frantic love.'

She rolls over then. I rest my hand on her back and feel her panting. The sharp, shallow breaths that only he could cause. She shuffles herself away to a cold patch of the mattress and is asleep in minutes.

I feel the veins in my neck tighten. I think of the therapist. How much are we paying her? Enough to live in that bizarre country house, to fund those ridiculous loose-leaf teas. And to what end? So that I can sit at night and listen while my wife cries herself to sleep? So that I can watch as she tosses and turns, endlessly calling his name?

Would there ever be an end to it, or was this

43

simply what we had been reduced to? A sad story you heard whispered about at dinner parties? A page you re-read perpetually, searching for an answer that would never come?

I thrash and twist until the sheets are wrapped round my body, slick with sweat, and then I tear them off me and skulk downstairs to the kitchen, where I pour myself a glass of water.

I hold it up to the light and consider throwing it through the window. I imagine ripping the cupboard doors off their hinges, hurling dinner plates into drywall, ripping apart plasterboard. I think about reducing the house down to its very foundation, to nothing. I imagine leaving, surveying the wreckage of my life with a growing distance and feeling a great relief. The act of destruction somehow constructive.

I grip the counter and take a moment to collect myself. When I turn the kitchen faucet off I'm surprised to find that I can still hear the sound of running water.

I open the cupboards beneath the sink and run my hands along the pipework but find them dry to the touch. I wander the house tightening faucet handles and checking radiator valves, but I can't spot any sign of a leak. When I eventually give up and slide back into bed, Simone stirs. The sound is somehow louder in our bedroom.

'Do you not hear that?' I ask her.

'Hear what?'

'I can hear running water.'

'You were probably just dreaming,' she says hazily.

But I haven't been to sleep.

XI

The television documents the growing crisis in Oregon in excruciating detail. I see videos of people in the late stages of the illness. Their bodies bloated, the whites of their eyes shot red, their faces engorged. Like an infant, the news cries out for attention, drowning out all conscious thought.

There are statistical projections, entire data models, that say the sick will soon outnumber the healthy. From a levee, I watch the storm waters rise. By midweek, when the hospitals become overrun, they begin bussing the sick away from the denser population centres. The government establish quarantine zones. They refer to the sites as 'staging areas' in an attempt to suggest a transitory effort, but the media are quick to label the locations ghettos.

I see shaky footage of a transport bus as it strikes a lamppost and veers into oncoming traffic. The driver is killed instantly and a fire is started which quickly spreads. The sick remain motionless as the flames rise up and begin to swallow them.

Before they are engulfed entirely they turn to face the spectators in the street. Through the grainy film it almost looks like they are smiling.

I watch the news late into the night and wake earlier each morning, tired as if my body is living a double life. I turn the lights low and wrap myself in a blanket in front of the television. When barren winter branches tap at the upstairs windowpanes I hold my breath, mistaking them for knocks at the front door.

I think often about the nameless weeping doctor, that poor unattributed soul. She is roughly the same age Simone had been when we first met. They share a similar complexion. I imagine that in another life they could be sisters, and in a moment of weakness I cut her photograph out of the paper and hide it between the pages of a book. When the house is quiet I sit and study it. With each viewing new details seem to emerge. I notice that she wears a heavy necklace, a black teardrop of stone that sits against her breastbone, and I imagine holding it in my hand.

When the military take control of hospitals throughout the state I search for her face in the swarming crowds. I scour the papers in hopes that she will appear in the background of a photograph. But as the press pull back, as members of the local government gradually succumb to the illness, I feel my hope begin to wane.

In San Francisco a cruise ship en route from

Kauai ignores hails and crashes into a dock. It has been at sea for only a few days. When authorities board the vessel they find it empty. Though the eight hundred souls onboard are officially reported missing, lost at sea, authorities note that not a single lifeboat has been used. The coastguard conducts a thorough search and rescue mission but there are no signs of survivors. They leave the ship in port, the hole in its hull yawning like a mouth, the vessel taking on water until eventually it keels over in the shallow water.

Within hours there are reports out of Oregon that the sick have begun to disappear. From the same dimly lit hotel room the press once again interview the nurse with no face. She says that existing medical staff have all been relieved of duty.

'They vanished one by one,' she says. 'You see it sometimes when a patient wanders from their beds. But they were nowhere to be found. We searched for hours. We checked surveillance footage. No one came in and no one walked out.'

She takes a small sip of water, her hands trembling, her face pixelated.

'I've never seen anything like it. I don't think anyone has.'

An entire hospital full of empty beds.

The bodies gone. Disappeared.

XII

I close Phineas's bedroom window each night before I turn in. I know that in the morning Simone will rise before me and open it again to let the air through. She dusts and vacuums his room religiously. She dresses the bed every few days as if she expects him to one day return to it. She tells me she can't bear for his things to smell stale.

I stand at his window and look at Phil and Helen's house, aglow in the dark, and remember the night we met them. Simone wore an auburn red dress and we took a hyacinth plant as a gift. I remember walking behind her on the cobbled stone path. It was the first time we'd got dressed up to go anywhere in months. Her cheeks were red from the cold and the snow reflected in her eyes. She was showing, but the bump was neat and from behind it seemed non-existent, a strange trick of the light. I remember wanting her so badly.

'Why are we here again?' I asked as we made our way up to the house.

'They know we're new to the area so they invited us.'

'Philip and…'

'Phil and Helen,' she said, turning to adjust my tie.

The front door was framed by these giant stone rabbits. They stood proud and alert, their ears elongated, pointing straight upwards. I ran my hand along one, expecting it to be smooth like marble, but the texture was rough. I couldn't figure out if they were classy or just bizarre. When the door opened I was still fondling one of them. My hand shot back and I smiled like a maniac.

'You like those?' Phil asked with a smile. He was classically handsome. He stood broad-shouldered in the doorway and raised a large hand to stroke at his chin. 'Jury is still out for me. Helen can't get enough of them, though, and they're certainly a conversation starter.'

'They remind me of *Alice's Adventures in Wonderland*.' Simone smiled, her nose wrinkling.

'Then that must make me the Mad Hatter,' Phil said, taking her hand and leading the two of us inside. 'Won't you please follow me *Through the Looking-Glass*?'

Inside, the house opened to a large circular reception area. It was immaculate. Warm light ran along the ceiling and fell like rain across the cream carpeting. A large staircase snaked along the curvature of the far wall. On the upstairs landing guests lingered, touching each other's arms and laughing.

'We've made a coatroom out of one of the guest rooms,' Phil said. 'May I?' And then he rested his large hands on her shoulders from behind. She thanked him, shrugging off her coat and letting it fall easily into his arms. For a moment I imagined the two of them undressing each other, both eager and hungry to be alone.

I was thankful when Helen appeared holding two champagne flutes and kissed Simone on the cheek. 'You made it,' she said. She wore an open-backed dress that accentuated her curves. Her lips were the brightest shade of red I had ever seen. I remember staring at the white of her teeth. How they shone like pearl. 'And this must be your husband?'

When Simone was offered one of the flutes she shook her head gently and rested a hand on her stomach.

'Oh no, of course,' Helen said. 'What was I thinking?'

The two headed to the kitchen for a softer beverage and I followed Phil upstairs to discard the coats. On the landing he introduced me to his teenage son, Josh, who stood awkwardly in a shirt and sweater vest that hung off his slender frame. I almost pitied him. He was at least a decade younger than anyone else at the party. His body was elongated, perched on the precipice of adulthood. He smiled and we both nodded as his father listed his various scholarly ambitions and extracurricular activities. I told him it was nice to have met him and he seemed relieved when his father nodded, giving him the go-ahead to slink off.

'Do you guys know what you're having?' Phil asked as we laid the coats down.

'A boy,' I said.

'Good,' he said. 'That's good. They're easier – until they aren't.'

When Phil took me on a tour of the house, I noticed his slacks were tailored to sit tightly round the curvature of his calves, whereas mine hung loose over my shoes; that my shirt was ill-fitting and bunched round the waist, whereas the lines of his were fitted. And I worried for a moment that I must have looked to him the way Josh did to me, like a child playing at being a man.

He explained that he worked in retail, although I later found out that he actually owned a chain of burgeoning boutique grocery stores across the Midwest. He also mentioned that he played a fair amount of sport in his college days, and it was only when we passed a wealth of trophies in his office that it became clear he had walked away from a professional career.

It didn't take me long to realise that his success and subsequent modesty was a recurring theme. What I struggled to determine, much like the stone rabbits, was whether it was genuine or a polished act, a false modesty.

Regardless, I found that I liked the man. He had an amiability that he could turn on and off in a way that was both benign and persuasive, and it wasn't until we circled round and met up with Simone and Helen that I realised I'd drunk perhaps a little too much.

When we returned to the coatroom at the end of the evening I pressed myself into Simone, running my hand up the length of her thigh. We kissed in the cool darkness, her lips wet and full, and I laid her down gently among the coats.

'We can't do this here,' she whispered.

'No one would know,' I said. 'It's been a while.'

She was silent for a moment, as if considering it. When I kissed her again she gently slid out from under me and straightened her dress.

'Come on, Casanova. My feet are killing me.'

When we got home she went upstairs to prepare for bed. By the time I made my way up she was asleep. I slid in beside her and kissed her cheek. I smelt her perfume and stared at the ceiling, listening to her shallow breaths. And when sleep failed to take me I touched myself in the dark and imagined her and Helen together, their lips red and alive, their bodies intertwined and writhing among all of those black coats.

XIII

All through the night I think I can hear the patter of rainfall, but outside the sky sits clear and cloudless. As I lie in bed I hear the sound of running water falling from somewhere high above me.

In my mind I imagine a loose roof shingle and a thin stream running along exposed decking, the liquid pooling among the loft insulation and sagging the boards above our heads. I imagine the roof collapsing over us. A torrent of water. Yet when I take a flashlight and inspect the attic, running my hand along the ceiling's protective membrane, it is dry to the touch. There are no water stains. No signs of any leak.

I descend the attic ladder and strain my ears in the darkness to try to pinpoint the source of the sound. I press myself against the cold of the wall and listen carefully, but it's no use.

From the garage I take a ladder and use it to check the gutters. I remove clumps of leaves and other debris, but not enough to cause any blockage.

I check the faucets again. I press my ear against toilet cisterns.

The longer I search for the source of the sound the more imperative its discovery becomes. I imagine a pipe bursting in the basement, the water rising until it is waist-high. I imagine sodden boxes floating on the black surface of the water. The remains of Simone's wedding dress and Phineas's toys. The keepsakes of our old life. Things we no longer have use for, but could never bring ourselves to part with.

I imagine landslides and earthquakes. Forest fires and tornadoes. I imagine the house reduced to rubble, to cinder, to ash. How easy it would be, I think, for an act of God to destroy our shared history. The thought turns in my stomach. It inches up my spine.

Upstairs I'm about to check the master bathroom when Simone emerges from the bedroom. 'What time is it?' she asks, one eye open, her hair tangled.

'It's late,' I say. 'I couldn't sleep. Go back to bed.'

She nods and turns back into the dark of the bedroom and I am almost tempted to follow her. To take her into my arms. To free us temporarily from the burden of our collective sadness. But the thought of touching her feels invasive. There is a distance between us that seems to grow with each passing day.

I stand in the hall and try desperately to will myself into action but by the time I turn in she's asleep. I strip down to my underwear and slide in beside her. From somewhere deep in the house the sound of running water continues unabated. I listen to it and feel an anger stirring inside of me. A great weight pressing on my skull.

I see Simone's shape in the darkness, her body rising and falling, and I know that I am losing her. That our relationship will one day be packed away, much like our keepsakes. A box in a basement somewhere.

Phineas's death was instantaneous, but ours would happen slowly, in gradual increments. Its stone foundation eroded over time by the gentlest of forces.

I imagine a tepid stream running like a vein beneath the house. I see thousands of microscopic cracks forming beneath our feet. A great sinkhole opening beneath us, the ground yawning to swallow the house. I see myself in the car, watching Simone from the rear-view mirror. She waves meekly as the walls fold round her and the smoke rises like steam to take her away.

XIV

We convene at the therapist's house once a week. Simone always manages to arrive before me. I see her standing against the black mass of the house. She looks thin, the lines of her face drawn, yet when I kiss her on the cheek I tell her otherwise. She has accused me in the past of sheltering her from truths, and perhaps that is why I feel such a sense of trepidation during our sessions. The house seems almost to demand honesty.

From her porthole window the therapist watches over us. We pass beneath the wooden beams of the veranda and we wait before the red door. I stare at the lion door knocker, running my finger along its bronze mane, the curvature of its face. I imagine for a moment that the rest of its body exists on the other side of the door. Its legs withered. The musculature of its back strained from carrying the weight of that ring in its mouth for the rest of eternity.

We are led through the house. We pass many doors. Some are open and I try desperately to peek inside.

The house is full of art. A truly enormous collection. In almost every room there are canvases hanging from walls, frames resting against bookcases, great stacks piled beneath dust sheets.

In one room I spot an enormous painting resting above a large marble fireplace. A pale blue gradient that runs down the length of the canvas and ends in the darkest colour I have ever seen. It is scarcely a colour at all but rather a total absence of light. My eyes follow its descent. It stops me in my tracks. I stand in the hallway and stare at it. I feel the darkness pulling at the edges of my mind. It's only when the therapist takes me gently by the shoulder that I allow myself to carry on.

We sit beneath a painting of the sea and talk about the weight of absence. How after the accident we had both begun to see the body of our own grief. We had watched as it was born, fusing bone and knitting skin. How over the course of several weeks it had come together in the shape not of a man, but of a boy. And how gradually it had taken residence in the house, bringing with it a furious anger.

Simone held a mirror to it, directing it squarely upon herself, whereas I projected it in great fits of rage that saw plates smashed and tables overturned. Now I seemed to carry it wherever I went. I felt it coursing through my body like an oil slick in my bloodstream.

My mother insisted that I had inherited my ˜mper as a sort of birthright. That I came from a long line of men completely incapable of getting out of their own way. Like my father, and his father before him, I had been saddled with it. A debt that I would never be able to repay, that I was ultimately destined to bestow upon my own children.

My father certainly hadn't been an easy man to live with. I remember incessant arguments between him and my mother. Small squabbles that would gradually escalate until you heard the front door slam and his car pulling out of the driveway. He would disappear for hours at a time, leaving behind the kind of silence that rang in the ears. Often I found my mother smoking silently at the kitchen table, staring out towards some imagined landmark.

He became an almost mythic creature in my young life, like a character from the comic books I read; I regarded him as a sort of subhuman. He was a creature relatable at a distance but alien under any sort of direct scrutiny. His motivations were indecipherable to me. When he slept did he dream of other lives? Did he harbour desire, I wondered, or was the idea of his own happiness as vague and abstract to him as it felt to me?

He lived and died a labourer. I was still a boy when he was formally diagnosed with mesothelioma. I'd been playing one morning when my mother sat with me and explained the cause of his illness. A tiny particle, she said, ingested on a worksite. A microscopic fibre that had lingered in his body, slowly going about its work.

As I sit and try to remember his face, the shape of his body, I realise my memory of him has been tainted by the symptomatology of his disease, the circumstances of his death. I see his clubbed fingertips. How his cough would rattle through him and wake me in the night. How I would lie still in bed and hear him wandering the halls, his wheezing breath like some terrible phantom.

I remember my parents arguing with increasing frequency towards the end. My mother sided with the doctors, who urged him to pursue palliative care, but the more she insisted the more he seemed to lean into his own fate. He would storm out of the house, gripping the roof of his car to steady himself, before vanishing.

The thought of his death was as terrifying to me as it was mesmeric. I refused to believe it was happening at all until I heard the din of their final argument. The familiar chorus of whispers that quickly whipped into a frenzy. I remember preparing myself. Waiting for the clapping of the front door, the way the picture frames would shake in the hall; but the sound never came. When I left my room I found my mother bent over him, swaddling him in a blanket. He'd been too weak to stand, and it was then that I realised a balance had shifted. He was gone a month later.

It's only when the therapist turns to me and asks, 'Is it possible that your anger is related to culpability? A subconscious allotment of blame?' that I begin to consider the eerie parallels between my parents' situation and our own. I think of all of the evenings spent watching Simone at the kitchen table, listless and forlorn. My furious outbursts and subsequent late-night drives.

It strikes me suddenly that loss is a process disguised as an event. We are consumed in our grief. We see only senselessness. But loss is gradual and seldom blameless. It is the result of thousands of events that interact at an almost imperceptible, microscopic level.

When Simone begins to weep beside me I take her hand in mine. She looks tired. I think of the day that he died. How I had shaken her awake on the beach towel. How it felt as though I'd been trying to shake her awake ever since.

'Phineas?' I asked her. 'Where is Phineas?'

I remember the panic in her eyes. The way she shot upright and asked, 'Is he not with you?'

I look at the therapist and grit my teeth.

'Phineas's death was an accident,' I say.

She had rested her eyes for a minute. It was a momentary lapse in judgement. But at night my body aches, my mind races. I see him wandering towards the shoreline and I ask myself *why, why, why?*

When she lay down was it a conscious decision?

When she closed her eyes did she feel herself slipping away?

Did she dream?

XV

I'm watching the news when the plumber arrives.

A list of yellow bullet points flashes across the screen. The newsreader states that authorities in Oregon have grounded air traffic and that the state borders have been closed. An infographic appears, showing landmass consumed by an acreage of growing red dots. It looks like an X-ray, an organ riddled with tumours.

I lead the plumber upstairs to the attic and explain the situation.

'Notice any stains or discolouration?' he asks, flicking the beam of his flashlight over pipework.

I shake my head no.

'Mould or mildew?'

When I shake my head again he puffs out his cheeks, rubs the fat at the back of his neck. 'Where'd you say you can hear it?'

'It's loudest upstairs. But it's intermittent.'

'Intermittent?'

'It doesn't happen all the time.'

'I know what intermittent means.' He sighs and tucks the flashlight into his waistband. He makes his way over to the boiler. 'You notice any drop in water pressure?'

'No,' I say. 'I mean, I haven't checked.'

'It's a closed system, so that'd be a good indicator,' he says. He pauses for a moment. 'An indicator is like a clue.'

'Yeah, thanks.'

The plumber rubs his chin. His forehead creases. 'Usually we get calls from folks when the water's up here,' he says, pointing to his neck. 'You mind if I take a look round downstairs?'

I leave him to his work and stand in the study. I've always found it difficult to relax with workmen in the house. I turn the television on, but leave it muted. I watch members of the National Guard rolling out barbed wire strips along a stretch of highway. Men with dogs patrolling a floodlit perimeter.

'You have any work done recently?' the plumber asks from the doorway, startling me.

'Not recently,' I say. 'Why?'

'There's signs of pretty extensive water damage on the staircase,' he says.

We walk together and he runs his finger along the skirting board. 'See how it fans out at the bottom there? Looks like the wallpaper's been replaced too. How long you had the place?'

'Six years or so,' I say.

'Well, you had a leak here at one point,' he says.

His phone rings and he apologises while he silences it.

'What do you suggest?' I ask.

'Always the same thing: treat the cause, not the symptom.'

'And in lieu of a cause?'

The plumber whistles, rocking back and forth on the balls of his feet. 'The problem is these things tend to be pretty localised, so it becomes a bit of a fishing expedition. I could put some sealant through the system, if it'd help put your mind at rest.'

'Failing that?'

'If there is a leak, and it's still an *if* at this point—'

'There's definitely a leak,' I say.

His phone rings again. He scrunches his face at the screen. 'It's my wife,' he says. 'Mind if I take this?'

He takes the call outside and I turn my attention back to the television. I see a convoy of busses pulling to the side of a country road. Their hydraulic doors open in unison, a grand choreographed spectacle that sees men in decontamination suits begin funnelling out the sick passengers. They walk like a chain gang into a makeshift compound, a shanty town of relief tents that look like white pustules against the landscape.

There is an efficiency to the process that feels obscene. There are too many bodies to count, let alone catalogue. They leave the busses as individuals only to become nameless beyond the walls of the compound. The scale of loss is unimaginable. I think for a moment about that poor, nameless doctor. I wonder if she is lost somewhere among the crowd.

The plumber returns and apologises for the interruption. 'We're expecting,' he says. You never know if the next call is going to be *the* call, you know?'

'If there's somewhere you need to be—'

He waves me away, watching the television. 'She wants me to do a grocery store run, if you can believe it. She's got a craving for popsicles, she says. In this weather.'

I smile politely.

'I don't envy you,' I say. I lie.

XVI

Simone never had cravings, but the pregnancy caused her terrible heartburn. I remember countless late-night drives for antacids and ingredients for other homemade remedies, like the apple cider vinegar she would sip or the baking soda she mixed with water. She took ginger and tried liquorice supplements, but nothing ever worked. It was his hair, she said. Something about the unique mixture of hormones that caused its excessive growth and upset the digestive tract. An old wives' tale, I thought. But she was always so apologetic when the pain became too much and she had to wake me in the night. She would rub circles into the small of my back as I fumbled in the dark for my wallet and keys.

And though I acted as if it were a great hardship, some valiant effort, I secretly enjoyed those late-night drives, when the roads were quiet and the world seemed vacant and uninhabited, as if it could be mine.

It was an escape from the monotony that had befallen the house, the strange gravity that had developed and turned us both into a satellite for the child. And though I was elated, it was difficult not to view the pregnancy as an act of reduction. I felt the beginnings of a great paradox in which I saw the reality of my own existence but also the absence of it. The more the child grew, the more I felt myself shrink.

I would stare out towards the city lights on those long drives, towards the shimmering of brake lights suspended on the freeway, and I would imagine Simone was beside me. That we were returning to our old apartment, to our old lives, our old bodies. As if we had woken up from some elongated fever dream, some stupor, and realised that we had betrayed ourselves. I felt the lights calling to me, but the effect was fleeting. The sudden blindness from the headlights of a passing car was enough to snap me back to reality.

I kept my growing disenchantment with the suburbs, with the changes we were experiencing, largely to myself because I knew that they would be temporary. That we would, in fact, return to ourselves, to our old lives, our old bodies, at least in part. That given time we would ultimately grow to inhabit better versions of ourselves.

I knew this because I saw a vision of our future in Phil and Helen. And on the weekends, when we would meet with them for drinks, I would stand outside on the patio with Phil, the two of us hovering over their exposed fire pit, and he would rub my shoulder and whisper me his counsel.

'Look at all that you have. A wife who adores you. A beautiful house. A stable job. People have killed for less,' he told me once, nursing a bourbon with a reverence that was lost on me. 'I know what your problem is,' he said, pointing a finger at me. 'You don't think you deserve it. You don't think anyone deserves it.'

'Deserves what?' I asked, chuckling, kicking a loose piece of firewood and watching as the embers rose into the cold night air.

'All of this,' he said, fanning his arms out. 'You think you have to make a choice. You think you have to make a sacrifice. But that's not true.' He stumbled over and wrapped an arm round me.

'You're drunk, Phil.'

'That doesn't mean I'm not right.'

He sat down then on a lawn chair, a thin layer of snow dampening the back of his shirt. Helen found us, carrying a blanket. 'What are you doing down there? You'll freeze.'

'We're putting the world to rights,' he said.

'I can see that,' she said. 'But maybe we should do that inside, where there's less of a wind chill?'

He reached for her then, pulling her down onto him and kissing her neck. She curled into his body and they lay together beneath the stars. Simone emerged from the kitchen and rested her head on my shoulder. I ran my hand along her bump and we stood in silence. Away from the congestion of the city the stars shone with a brilliance that I felt I would never get used to.

Eventually Phil clambered to his feet and made a beeline for the house. I watched him leave with a sense of admiration that surprised me. Though I found him extravagant, sometimes forced, I felt that at heart he was an honest man. His life, the balance he'd been able to strike between his personal and professional commitments, the way he conducted himself, gave me a certain hope for my own future.

'Keep him away from open flame,' I called out to Helen as we left. 'He's got enough bourbon in him to take the whole neighbourhood with him.'

XVII

I sit alone and watch news of the pandemic. It has little to do with fear, I tell myself, more a sort of morbid curiosity. The media blackout caused by the cordon sanitaire in Oregon is now almost total. What little there is to be seen is reported out of Washington, Nevada and Idaho, where new outbreaks are reported daily. It's only a matter of time, they say, before California sees its first victim.

Despite its virulence little is known about the disease. They say that it attacks the brain and spinal column. That victims suffer encephalitis-like reactions. Lethargy, confusion and changes in personality are all common. The media report cases of grandiose delusions and memory loss. Some hear voices, others see impossible realities. All eventually disappear.

On message boards and social networks, amateur footage circulates of a Hispanic woman in the terminal stages of the disease. She sits at home, the whites of her eyes filled with blood. The skin of her forehead wrinkled and loose, the flesh beneath swollen and bulbous, as if from some horrific allergic reaction.

Her face looks as though it is spreading, pulling apart to blossom like the petals of a flower. A voice calls out to her from behind the camera and she smiles, her head lolling towards the sound, her red eyes frantic. When she reaches out her daughter takes her hand and cups it in hers. I stop watching then. She is a mother. She is someone's child.

The disease, from what I can find online, has three distinct phases.

First, in the prodromal stage, comes the fever. The body rattles as the illness burns through it, and in the confusion the mind retreats inward, to the sanctuary of dreams.

In the second phase, the acute stage, reality begins to phase in and out. Carriers experience auditory and visual hallucinations as their dream state begins to coalesce with reality. It's then that the blood vessels in the eyes burst and the face mushrooms outward.

The final stage, the act of disappearance, is so poorly documented that I fail to find a single accurate source of information about it online, though there are rumours. Frenzied speculation.

People post en masse to message boards.

'Where are the bodies?' they ask. 'What of the dead?'

Others hypothesise endlessly over the nature of the disease and its source. They discuss portals of entry and modes of transmission. Is it like mononucleosis, the kissing disease? Something spread by acts of outward affection? They talk of the illness's virulence. Conspiracy theorists preach about weaponised bacterial strains and false flag attacks. Others discuss zoonosis and the animals that could be helping to propagate the virus.

I follow their links and I fall down the rabbit hole of armchair expertise. I read late into the night about the chains of infection that have led to past epidemics.

Nature, I discover, is astonishingly inventive in its cruelty.

First a reservoir is discovered, a source. In the case of Guinea-worm disease this is a body of water containing tiny microscopic parasites called copepods. The infected copepods carry the Guinea-worm larvae inside of them. When a human drinks from the water supply they ingest the copepods, which promptly die in the stomach and release the infectious larvae into the body. Within ten months the larvae mature and develop into three-foot worms that are as long and wide as spaghetti noodles. When they are ready to emerge a blister forms on the skin, usually on the ball of the foot, or the flesh of the lower leg, but sometimes on the head. From there the worm writhes beneath the skin for three unbearable days before the blister bursts and the worm uncoils and hangs from the ulcer like a piece of string. When the worm comes into contact with water it releases a milky cloud containing millions of immature larvae, contaminating the new water source and further propagating the disease.

I follow link after link, watching as they turn from muted blue to purple. I open hundreds of tabs in my browser. In the dark of my office I traverse the sickly history of humanity. From the Black Death to avian influenza and Ebola. I look at pictures of swollen lymph nodes, inguinal bubo, skin lesions and acral gangrene. I see more mass graves than I thought possible. Entire cities of the dead built beneath our feet.

That night I sleep a troubled sleep.

I dream that Phineas is standing waist deep in a stream when the current sweeps his legs out from under him. He battles to keep his head above water as I stand on the bank and reach out to him. He calls my name, but as I stretch my fingers towards him a thousand worms burst from every surface of my body. When they touch his skin his body breaks down into clumps of cloudy liquid that sink down beneath the surface of the water, breaking apart and disappearing entirely in the surf. And as I cry out the worms rise up and flow down my throat, stifling my screams.

XVIII

I wake with a start, the landscape of our bedroom alien in the darkness. I use a thin trickle of light to acclimate myself. I make out the shape of our comforter, the four posters of our bed frame. Slowly reality slides into place. Truth presents itself.

Between a crack in the curtain dust motes dance in the air. I watch as they pile up on the carpet and settle on furniture. I remember, briefly, that the dead cells of the epidermis are one of the major constituents of household dust. That we shed more than half our body weight over the course of a lifetime. I consider how strange it is that even now, months after his death, Phineas still walks among us. He floats in the air. He brushes our skin. We carry him in our bodies.

I lumber out of bed and slip into the bathroom. I reach into the medicine cabinet and inspect the floral bag out of habit. I turn the pill bottle over in my hand. I read Simone's name off the label. I pour the pills onto my palm and perform a crude inventory but the count is always the same.

I know that the discovery is likely of no real significance. A prescription filled hastily at the height of her grief. Medication she no longer has any real use for, that she has probably forgotten entirely. But I feel such a sense of foreboding when I hold the bottle. It is as if I have uncovered the existence of a clandestine life. A reality from which I am totally isolated.

Simone struggled briefly with sleep during her pregnancy but an obstetrician assured us it was quite normal, nothing that would require medical intervention. It was discomfort, rather than insomnia. She was sure that Phineas was trying to expedite his own delivery. He would press on her bladder in the night and she would pace in the hall, full of a nervous energy. I remember waking often to find her missing, her body reduced to a cold spot on the bed.

She would take long baths. It was the only thing that seemed to soothe the both of them, and it was there that her waters had finally broken and she had called out my name in the darkness.

I helped her dress and gathered up the bags she had packed so carefully. She sat on the couch, clutching her stomach, and tried her best to relay instructions between laboured breaths.

'Don't forget the orange bag. The one with the babygrows.'

'You can barely stand,' I said, stroking her hair. 'Would you please stop trying to micromanage this?'

She placed her arm over my shoulder and I helped her to the door.

'Wait,' she said, 'wait.'

We stood over the threshold. 'What's wrong?' I asked.

'This will be the last time it's just the two of us,' she said. 'When we come back here, it'll be with him.' It felt ridiculous to admit but I hadn't considered it. The pregnancy had occupied so much of our cognitive energy that I hadn't given a single thought to what came afterwards. To the result of the pregnancy. To the fact that we would share our home with a third party. That our lives would become his.

When panic sent a fresh wave through the waters of my body I kissed her on the forehead and said, 'Can we please go now?'

The roads were empty in the storm winds. Through the sheets of rain that lashed the windscreen and the gusts that rocked our little car we saw the world one heartbeat at a time. I remember the landscape around us looked like black waves in the darkness.

We are all just ships at sea, I thought, tiny vessels.

And when we reached the hospital she waded into the waters of the birthing pool and I watched as he was born beneath them. I held him in my arms and he screamed into the freezing air, his tiny body shivering.

They both slept while the sun rose. I remember how the room filled with a cold yellow light. And when the doctor discharged her I placed Phineas in his car seat and fumbled with the straps, and as we made our way past the nurses' station and out towards the elevators I waited for someone to stop us. For a doctor to take the child into his arms and scold the two of us. Because surely there had to be some kind of orientation? Some aptitude test. A questionnaire we were required to fill in and return, some examination we had to pass before they let us take a life out into the world. But when no one came we filed into the elevator and then out into the car park, and with each footstep we were changed.

I remember the first song that played on the radio as I took the two of them home. And how I held him in those first weeks as if he were a small bird, his bones hollow, his body impossibly weak. I remember Simone in a dressing gown dancing with him in the kitchen. I remember bathing his pink and wrinkled body. I remember a tiredness so consuming that I could taste the blue of electricity. I remember laughter, too, but it has vanished now into the hollow spaces of my mind.

I see only the fleeting shadow of it.

XIX

Simone grows increasingly restless throughout the final days of winter. She is keen for the frost to recede, for spring to arrive so that she may venture outside. Each morning she takes her coffee and edges a little further into the garden, as if she is trying to ward off the cold. Like a child chasing waves up and down the shoreline, it becomes a sort of ritual.

She spends her time planting tomatoes and peppers in the kitchen. It is a surprisingly delicate process. She sows the seeds into specialised pots, filling them with a sterilised soil mixture to facilitate growth before placing the trays beneath grow lights and labelling each diligently. There are disease-resistant strains, determinate and indeterminate varieties, all manner of fertiliser compounds.

We seldom speak. It seems the longer we are together the less our conversations require words at all. Her body speaks to me in its proximity. I am uniquely attuned to it. I read her objections out of the air. I try to take comfort in old adages.

I tell myself that she needs time, that her work in the garden will be a welcome return to normalcy. That this will all soon pass.

She had always been prone to fits of isolation. Before the accident I would return often to find her waiting for me on the stairs, her body perched as if over some invisible edge. Desperate for either adult conversation or simply a break from tending to the needs of a toddler. When he had been particularly impetuous she would hand over the baton like a relay runner, without speaking a word, and disappear upstairs to lie prostrate on the cool of our bed until it was time to bathe him.

'I must have picked these things up a hundred times today,' she said one evening as we crawled on all fours across the playroom floor. 'I feel like Sisyphus.'

'Find me a rock that looks as cute as he does in a pair of dungarees.'

'I'm serious,' she said.

'He's a child.'

'Very observant,' she said, sitting up and pressing her palms against her eyelids. She sighed. 'I get to the end of days like this and I think what have I accomplished?'

'You're doing an incredible job.'

'It doesn't feel like progress.'

'You don't see him the way I do. You're too close to it. I leave early for work. Sometimes I'm home after bedtime. I'll go two or three days without any time with him and then on the weekends the change is incredible. It's like passing a construction site every morning. It's this skeleton of timber for months and months and then one day you drive by and there's just this beautiful, pristine building. You sit in the shadow of it and you think: where did this come from?'

'I know,' she said, biting the skin round her nails, tearing it off in thin strips, her voice distant. 'I know.'

'Do you want to go back to work?' I asked.

She was silent for a long time. We both sat and watched the question turn stale in the air between us. I realised then that the answer was yes. That she missed work terribly, but was too ashamed to admit it. Financially we could survive on my salary, which meant, at least in her mind, that a return to work would equate to failure. An admittance that Phineas's love alone could not sustain her. A ridiculous notion that she herself was somehow bankrupt, devoid of the compassion that women such as Helen, who had stayed at home full-time, were clearly so capable of.

'No,' she said finally. 'No. He's too young to leave.'

She decided instead that she would embark on a series of home renovations: painting and wallpapering the upstairs rooms while he slept, remodelling the kitchen and, perhaps her favourite of all, transforming the garden.

She planted multi-tiered beds of ornamental

grass, blue fescue, lily turf and Japanese sedge, which would sway in the breeze and give the impression that the house was a boat at sea. From auction websites she found antique bird boxes and feeders, which she elevated on poles and lined along a gravel path bordered by black-eyed Susan and phlox.

On the porch she hung a wooden swing so that Phineas could sit outside and eat lunch while the insects and wildlife teemed round him. And at the foot of the garden, at the end of the gravel path, she built a vegetable patch, which over the course of several years she taught him to harvest.

It was only after school began that Simone allowed herself to return to work. I remember thinking then how fortunate I had been to have been born a man. To be able to live as the breadwinner not by discussion or election, but by assumption. I knew that I would never have been able to bear staying home in the way that she had. And though I had always insisted that Simone was free to decide whether she returned to work or not, I would have been lying if I'd said her decision hadn't benefitted me greatly. That by sheer grace of my gender I had avoided that messy discussion, that sad admittance that being a father alone would never have been enough to satisfy me completely.

XX

The illness burns like a fever along the northwest coast, its tendrils slowly creeping inland. The government repurposes arenas and sport centres as quarantine zones. They erect roadside checkpoints. They build firebreaks by evacuating entire neighbourhoods, yet still the illness spreads. Weeks pass. Each day new outbreaks are reported. Rioting and violence follow the announcements like a chemical stain.

By early summer the flames have crossed entire states. We begin to feel the radiant heat. It bears down on us, the air close as if our bodies have been wrapped in cellophane. Despite assurances that the sickness isn't airborne, people leave their houses wearing respirator masks. Deliveries become less frequent. I see squad cars parked outside of local grocery stores.

Footage airs out of Dallas of a young boy walking naked down a gridlocked highway, his face and limbs bloated as if from some horrific allergy. The whites of his eyes turned red from subconjunctival haemorrhaging. Simone and I watch the broadcast in abject horror. It looks as if his entire body is burning from within.

He stumbles and lurches forward over the asphalt before finally falling to his knees. He places his hands in his lap and lifts his head towards the sky. His body relaxes and for a brief moment he seems peaceful, contemplative.

'The following footage may be too sensitive for young viewers,' the telecaster warns.

The boy smiles at the horrified onlookers as his ashen skin grows pale, as it begins to separate from his body. It slides down his slender frame and quickly vanishes to expose the gelatinous fat beneath, the slick white tension of his subcutaneous tissue. Then the musculature of his body melts away to reveal his skeleton, the internal organs beneath.

He looks as if he is a living anatomical figurine.

I watch his heart as it sends fresh blood screaming round his body. It seems furious, as I suppose most caged things are. I kneel in front of the television and feel my chest tighten. I touch the screen, tracing the shape of the boy, and feel the crackle of electricity at my fingertips.

I watch as his skeleton disappears. As the internal machinery of his body is disassembled. Until his brain is all that is left, suspended in mid-air. The intricate network of nerves connected to it hanging down like the roots of a plant.

The camera shakes as bystanders begin to flee the

scene in panic. People abandon their vehicles and surge forward, a great mass of bodies. By the time the footage stabilises the transformation is complete and the boy is gone. He has vanished completely.

In the wake of the broadcast the authorities assure the public that the illness is being contained, that the measures they have put in place are working. They ask for patience and trust. But each day state lines seem to grow dimmer, eroded by the infection's lashing waves. The illness leaves only land in its wake. Vast expanses of unoccupied geography.

The media is unable to reach consensus on what to call the missing. Many outlets refer to them simply as 'the disappeared'. In the absence of bodies they are treated more like captives than casualties. Various religious denominations claim the acts as divine intervention. Others see it as an act of war. The world's militaries perform drills. They fire aimless missiles into international waters and march in impotent formations. Submarines and warships dance endlessly in the Pacific.

A group of religious spokesmen scale the White House gates and are tackled by Secret Service agents. A state senator is assassinated outside a town hall meeting. The president begins daily televised broadcasts urging the public to remain calm.

A congregation in Utah hold hands and drink in unison from styrofoam cups. Parents lift the chins of their sons and daughters to help the mixture down. When the cameras pull back to show their slumped bodies I'm reminded of the painting in our therapist's office. A calm sea. Clouds looming on the horizon.

Shaky footage circulates online of a group of urban explorers documenting their journey deep into the heart of the quarantine zone. In the streets the wind whistles as it passes through lanes of empty cars, echoing as it bounces off looted storefronts. They scale the stairwell of an office building and shoot a panoramic view of the city from the roof. Pillars of smoke rise high into the sky all around them, and though they call out there isn't another living soul for miles. Within a week they post a video update. Half of them are sick with the illness. Their faces bloated, their eyes shot red.

In a matter of hours they too will be gone.

XXI

'I think a lot about that poor boy on the highway,' Simone says during our next session. She's not alone. I think about it in the twilight before sleep takes me. His skin as thin as parchment. His furious heart. 'It's such a terrible way to die,' she says.

'Is that what you think is happening?' the therapist asks.

Simone fumbles with her hands. 'I don't know.'

'Is it death, I wonder, or is it a metamorphosis?'

'A metamorphosis?'

'Is it truly outside the realm of possibility that the illness is not destroying the mind at all, but rather transmuting the body?'

'Is that not a kind of death?' I ask. 'The end of one existence in exchange for the beginning of another?'

I try to imagine the act of disappearance as a phase transition. That the dead are transmuting their bodies to become part of some shared, communal consciousness. But it feels like science fiction. I think of metempsychosis.

The concept of reincarnation. The seemingly endless redistribution of cosmic energies.

'Saprotrophic nutrition,' the therapist says. 'That's what they call it in nature. The concept of one life nourished by the death of another.'

'So you do believe it's a kind of death?' Simone asks.

'I believe it depends on your definition of a person.'

'My father used to say that people were the sum of the choices they made,' Simone says.

'Do you agree?' the therapist asks.

'I believe that a person is a house occupied by those they have met and loved. That in order to live a person must parcel themselves up and give parts of themselves away. To be carried by others and to live elsewhere, in other houses,' Simone says.

I close my eyes and wonder, like so many others, where the dead go.

There was a time when I took solace in the belief that our existence would be perpetuated by Phineas's memory of us. That we would continue to live long after death in his collective past. But now I feel only a terrible burden. Our intimacies seem inextricable. I alone carry parts of him, just as Simone carries her own remembrances. Pieces of him will be lost with us, just as pieces of us were lost with him.

I think for a moment about the day he lost his first tooth.

He had been young, too young to lose a tooth.

He fell up the staircase and it came loose on the hardwood. There was so much blood my knees felt weak. I remember how he held it in his hand. He thought it was bone, some integral part of him, and he pleaded with me to take him to a doctor.

I tried to comfort him.

'It had to come out eventually, to make room for your adult teeth,' I told him, and he nodded his head, but I could tell that he was lost in his anxiety. I could see it in his eyes, because they were Simone's eyes.

Eventually she came home and scooped him into her arms. She kissed his cheeks, still fat from early childhood, and told him all about the tooth fairy. Then the two of them went upstairs to place the white sliver beneath his pillow. I stood in the kitchen and heard the birdsong of their conversation, voices distant and muffled.

I remember how much it frustrated me that I could never soothe him the way that she could. I approached his problems with a cold logic, an efficiency that always seemed lost on him. It led often to frustration on my part and created a distance between us that I could feel growing. A hardening of our relationship.

I watched later from the doorway as Simone lifted the pillow beneath him and swapped the tooth for a coin. A token of youth.

I can still see the shape of her body in the dim light of that night. She seemed almost to float, like she was made of air. She asked me in the hallway what I thought we should do with it. It felt wrong to throw it away. But did we really want to keep it?

I can't remember what we did with it, in the end.

Maybe she bought a little ceremonial box and kept it as a trinket.

Maybe we flushed it like a dead goldfish.

Or maybe I walked it into the woodland behind the house and covered it with a shallow mound of dirt.

The horrible truth of the past is that our memories are organic. They ripen and sour. They transform with each recollection. I remember the beginning of his life and the end of it. The two moments coalesce to inhabit the same space in my mind, and in that way my memory of him is stained, and by extension so too is his life.

I begin to think that perhaps that is all a person really is: a practiced story, a performance refined with each retelling.

When I open my eyes Simone turns to the therapist and says, 'I believe there are parts of yourself that you give away temporarily, that can return to you, and there are parts that you must forfeit in perpetuity. There are places a person can go that they simply cannot return from.'

XXII

In the silence of our bedroom my history reduces to the rooms I remember most clearly throughout my life. They come together to form a house I don't recognise. An uncertain geography.

I walk through my childhood bedroom treading water. The carpets sodden. The wallpaper pockmarked and water-stained. I follow the sound of running water through my parents' living room and then up, into my college dorm room.

Somewhere deep in the belly of the house I can hear Simone crying out, calling his name and then mine in an endless cycle. I call back and continue to search for her.

I walk through the bedrooms of ex-girlfriends. Through the offices and kiosks of long-forgotten summer jobs. Through department store stockrooms and doctors' offices. Through classrooms and library stacks.

I find her standing in an overflowing bathtub, legs wet up to her knees, her face bloated as if from some horrific allergy. The whites of her eyes shot red and enflamed. Her tears falling in a solid sheet, filling the bathtub and spilling over perpetually.

She reaches out to me. Her hand hovering over the lip of the tub, over some imaginary precipice.

'Phineas?' I ask. 'Where is Phineas?'

'Is he not with you?' she asks.

Then she retches, bringing up black water. I can smell the salt in the air. It's invasive, almost overpowering. I walk backwards and shut the door behind me, but the scent lingers. It follows me. I feel heavy, as if I've been saturated by it somehow. A carrier for some imperceptible foreign body. I double over and vomit, each heave bringing up handfuls of the same water. It's only then that I realise the smell is coming from within me. That we are both sick with it. The same guilt.

And though I can't remember waking in the morning I feel more conscious than I have ever been. Simone rolls over to face me, and for a horrifying moment I expect to find her head bloated, her eyes shot red. But she is unchanged.

'I dreamt we were at sea,' she says.

XXIII

I hear running water all through breakfast. Each time I swallow, like a whisper. The sound disappears for long stretches, but inevitably it returns. There are minutes, hours, entire days when I hold my breath and wait. There is no measurable rhythm, no discernible pattern. I hear it so often it begins to sound like language. Sometimes the droplets fall rapidly, in enraptured speech, but often the breaths between are stuttered.

One grey afternoon I remember the book we bought Phineas on Morse code and find it on his bookshelf. I sit with a notepad in the kitchen and try to decipher the patterns, to translate them, but it is nonsense. When Simone arrives home I tear apart the pages out of embarrassment.

I walk the house with my fingers to walls as if I expect to feel a current beneath them. Sometimes I enter rooms and see puddles of water collecting on the hardwood floors but when I stop to inspect them I realise they are just pools of sunlight.

I put headphones on in the study and listen to records, but it brings me little peace. I realise I am listening more for the silence between tracks than the tracks themselves. I take long aimless drives, but when I return the sound greets me like an old friend.

I begin checking the faucets each night before I sleep. I tighten first the cold and then the hot water, placing my hand beneath each and counting to ten before checking the next. It becomes a ritual. I repeat the process until my skin aches, until blisters form. I chant to myself: left, right, left, right, and if I am interrupted I begin again.

I drag Simone from room to room. I have her press her ears to walls.

'You can't hear that?' I ask her, but she just shakes her head.

No, no.

'I'm sorry,' she says.

I try to rationalise the happenings. I tell myself that her hearing must be failing. I remind her that in our old apartment she could never hear our elderly neighbour. How each night his snores would carry through the walls of our bedroom.

'I believe you,' she says. But when she turns her hand over and places it against my forehead, checking my temperature in the way a mother would, I push her away.

'I'm not sick,' I tell her.

'I didn't say you were,' she says.

I storm up to the en-suite and run myself a cold

shower. The water takes the air from my lungs, the cold like a thousand fists along the length of my back.

I imagine Simone in the kitchen watching a news bulletin on the sickness. Reading the tip line number off the screen and dialling it to report my symptoms. I see an unmarked van appearing in the late afternoon and men in surgical masks running up the driveway to take me away.

I stop the shower, open the door and lean into the hallway. I listen for her muffled voice but the house is silent. I close the door and sit on the floor, my body warm against the freezing tiles.

'This is ridiculous,' I say.

It's then that I hear running water. Louder than usual. Heavier.

I look up to see that the shower is still dripping. I step in and wrench the handle down. In my anger I try to pull it off the wall but I slip on the wet ground and smash my knee into the floor. I cry out and punch at the wall. A small piece of tile chips away and a cut forms across the skin of my knuckles.

I hold my balled fist and watch as my blood mixes with the water at my feet. It creates spiral patterns that circle the drain and then disappear. I squeeze the wound and watch as fresh droplets fall and spread.

I've seen this before, I think.

I've seen this before.

XXIV

We continue with the sessions, though they seem increasingly futile. The television shows the same montage on endless repeat. Looted storefronts, tower blocks ablaze. Bodies jumping en masse from bridges. Crowds surging and being pushed backwards at international airport terminals. The deafening chorus of impassioned and as yet unanswered prayers.

In the car I listen to a telephone interview with a young girl trapped deep inside the quarantine zone. She says her parents are upstairs dreaming. That she will soon be dreaming too.

'There is no more darkness,' she says. 'Because when I close my eyes a thousand more open. The light cast through each falls upon me and I see into them like the keyholes of doors. I see my parents. I see how they were before me. I know them from before they even knew themselves.'

When I arrive at the therapist's house I pass beneath the property's large iron gates and I ascend the gravel path. I look for Simone against the black mass of the property but she is absent. From the porthole window I see the therapist. She smiles at me and for the first time descends the staircase before I can knock on the red door.

We walk together through the house and I am surprised to find that not a single door is closed. I see paintings of empty buildings. A forest of swaying pine trees turned upside down, their tips reaching into the blue of either ocean or sky. I see a field of rabbits, their ears extended.

We sit beneath a churning sea, separated by timid silence. I try to reach Simone on her cellphone multiple times but there is no answer. When it becomes clear she won't be attending, the therapist rises and begins to steep a pot of tea.

'This isn't like her,' I say, apologising profusely, making all manner of excuses.

I had spent months insisting that our visits were unnecessary, that Simone simply needed time to collect herself. But her absence today feels like an open admission, proof of a deeper dysfunction.

'I notice that she has seemed more withdrawn lately,' the therapist says.

It's not just during our sessions. At home I talk to fill the empty spaces her silence creates. It is a strange sort of inversion, a reversal of our before lives, where I had been raised to bottle emotions and she insisted on shining a chlorine light upon them. *Never go to bed angry* had been her campaign slogan in the early years of our relationship, and she had repeated it often. But silence was itself a sort of argument. We had reached an impasse, I felt, a stalemate. I attended the sessions as a means of keeping her hope alive, in an attempt to facilitate a change in her, but she spent them treading lightly. Now, it seemed, she was refusing to attend at all.

'This could be fortuitous,' the therapist says, setting down a cup and saucer in front of me. 'I'd been hoping to talk with you alone. To discuss Simone. You've mentioned on several occasions that you're unhappy with the progress we've been making.'

I nod my head and watch as the therapist fills the small china cup.

'You feel as though she is stuck. That her grief has destabilised her. That it has reopened childhood wounds,' the therapist says.

'She makes no attempt to get better.'

'It is natural, when watching a loved one suffer, to try to motivate them. But it's important to remember that depression is not a purely mental state. It is not laziness or weakness. The body is at work. It experiences biochemical changes. Patients suffer vegetative symptoms. Their sleep cycle is interrupted, their appetite diminished. The body is flooded with stress hormones. It becomes a war zone.'

I lean forward and place my head in my hands. I imagine Simone as a soldier on some distant shore and myself as a war widow, waiting impatiently by the phone. Praying for a letter that says she is finally coming home.

'I'm not ignorant to the fact that she is grieving. We are both grieving. But this melancholia refuses to lift. She refuses to even consider the possibility that it could.'

The therapist shifts in her seat. She points to an antique anatomical bust on the windowsill. 'Melancholia, as you call it, germinates in the mind, but it blossoms in the body. We suffer a loss and we fixate on that loss. We carry it with us. The ones we love urge us to move on, but their encouragement only seeks to further compound our sense of guilt. In a sense we mourn not only our loss, but the loss of our control over the situation, over our ability to repair the damage we have caused.'

I stare at the teacup in front of me. I think of the unending disappeared. The men, women and children all over the country who will be forced to watch their loved ones vanish. Their eyes red, their heads engorged.

'This can have disastrous consequences,' she says.

I close my eyes and reopen them. The upper half of my body feels weightless, but my feet feel impossibly heavy. I feel a thin current of air sweeping over my ankles. I reach to touch it but it whistles through the door and blows out into the hall.

'Do you understand?' the therapist says, her breathing hard, expectant.

I hear the draught upsetting doors in the hallway. The therapist winces as each slams shut. I feel the floorboards moving beneath my feet, the thunderous sound rippling throughout the house.

'Do you understand?' she says again, reaching out to place her hand upon mine.

'I'm sorry,' I say. 'I'm sorry.'

I wrench my arm back and get to my feet. She makes no effort to stand as I stumble into the hallway. I move quickly through the house, a maze of closed doorways, its hallways darkening second by second, and I am in my car before I know it. The therapist stands at the porthole window and watches as I pull away. I drive aimlessly round backroads until my breathing subsides, and then I head home.

I find Simone at the kitchen table. She stands to greet me and I can tell that she has been crying. It is strange, I think, how rarely we look at the people closest to us. If you were to ask me to draw Simone from memory I would describe her as she was on the day we first met. But as she stands before me now I realise she is older than I imagine her to be. She seems to have changed almost invisibly.

I reach out to steady her, my trembling hands drawing her body close as if the faintest breeze is all it would take to carry her away. We stand together. Our memory fragile, our time passing.

XXV

That night sleep steals me away like a thief. I hear distant thunder before I go. The sound of hurried feet on hardwood flooring. I think for a moment that the house is being overrun. I feel a panicked rash of sweat emerge across my body, but I find that I am unable to move. Though I'm still faintly aware of the stifling heat and stillness of our bedroom, I find myself biblically cold.

I see water all around us. We are at the beach, I realise. I shake Simone awake.

'Phineas? Where is Phineas?'

'Is he not with you?' she asks, sitting bolt upright on her beach towel.

The sun sits so low in the sky that it feels as though it's resting on my back. I walk the length of the beach. I call his name in a calm, measured voice. I walk until the beachgoers thin. Until the patchwork of towels dwindles. I walk until there is nothing but sand, and then I start back. I walk until I begin to run. Until my rising panic can no longer be hidden. Until the helter-skelter of my voice betrays me.

I shout his name. I ask strangers if they've seen him. I try to imagine his face, to condense his likeness. I try to recapitulate him into existence, as if he might manifest before my very eyes. But in my terror the edges of my memory begin to fray.

'Has anyone seen my boy?' I ask the faceless crowd. 'A young boy. Blond hair. About this high. Anyone? Please?'

Simone and I cross paths multiple times. Each time she appears her face is somehow a shade paler, as if she is fading from existence. We double over to look beneath beach loungers. We investigate sand dunes and the holes dug by other children. Strangers join in the search. People run back and forth between lifeguard towers. They blow whistles and order people out of the water.

When I hear the first screams, when I see the crowd swell and head up the beach towards some unseen commotion, I tell myself it must be unrelated.

Phineas is a smart boy.

He's always been comfortable near the water.

He wouldn't just wander off like this.

I keep telling myself all of this as I pry apart the shoulders of the teenaged onlookers and wade into the water to find his body floating in the shallows. His eyes open beneath the waves, staring up at me. And when I lift him up I'm reminded of the day he was born. A water birth. A beautiful boy.

I call out for Simone as I lay him down on the sand and try to clear his airway. I reason with him. I bargain. I beg.

Don't do this. Please.

I need you to breathe.

There are hundreds of people around me, but I am alone. For the first time in my life I feel true helplessness. In that moment I am a weak, broken thing. A child. I scan the crowd for any sign of an adult. For an authority figure, a badge, a uniform. Anyone capable of reversing the fate unfolding before me.

I ask for space as the crowd surges forward and blots out the sun, but I realise it's Simone. She stands over me, her head bloated. The whites of her eyes the colour of fire and change. She runs her hand down the back of my neck and pulls me close to her.

'He could be with us forever,' she whispers and I feel her tongue on my neck. It is lizard rough and the sensation reminds me of a childhood diving accident. A piece of fire coral that cut straight through my diving suit and left my blood to hang in the water like a cloud.

I push her away and reach for Phineas but both he and the crowd have disappeared. When I stand it is late winter, the beach windswept and empty. Simone wades into the water and lies down, submerging herself beneath the waves. She calls out to me before she disappears completely.

'Come,' she says. 'Lie with us.'

XXVI

Our grief is like a kaleidoscope through which we see our own history.

A lens that looks backwards through time.

I remember all of the newspaper headlines that have ever taken my breath away. So many of them involve children. They visit me in the night as glowing light. I see them forgotten in hot cars, lost and found too late in chest freezers, face down in bathtubs. I see them travelling along a desolate plain, a great restless mass. They walk forever lost between two great houses. I see Phineas now among them. His clothing ragged, his body filthy. A boy conceived of one mistake and dead as the result of another.

We, his parents, the complicit, are the sole survivors of his personal tragedy. In our silence we endlessly reconstruct the timeline of his final hours.

We ask ourselves *what if, what if, what if?*

We know that others will read our story and pass their judgement. We are marked by the official inquiry into his death. Condemned eternally in the court of public opinion. We imagine how friends and co-workers, even casual acquaintances, react to the news. How they gasp and shake their heads behind closed doors. How their voices soften and their bodies hunch as they discuss our personal tragedy.

Those poor people, they say.

Can you possibly imagine?

It's awful. But if you were that tired why would you ever let yourself lie down?

I know, I know.

Would you take your eyes off—?

Of course not.

That poor woman.

But where was his father? I hear them whisper. Where was his father?

It was piousness, I told myself, a means of coping with the shock of the event. The quiet personal assurance that such a thing could never happen to them. But Simone carried the weight of their imagined judgements. She felt the accident had turned her into a cautionary tale. She felt the radiant glare of a thousand downcast eyes.

She had been a wonderful, attentive mother. She had raised a beautiful son. He was courteous, polite, personable. You could see it in the outpouring of grief after his death. In the masses that stood overflowing the church parking lot as we arrived with him in the hearse. In the ceremony they held at his school and the quotes from neighbours and teachers that appeared in local newspapers and on television.

I approached the problem, as ever, with a cold logic. Surely, I reasoned, it wouldn't be possible for Phineas to have touched so many lives if we had failed him? Was this not empirical evidence of our success? But Simone simply couldn't see it. She believed that she had failed him. That she would continue to fail him.

In her grief she built a monument to him. A grand marble structure that reflected the world all around. And with each passing day it grew taller, more perfect in her mind. But as its beauty increased so too did the nature and severity of her sin, until it became a tower that she could never look away from. She saw it looming constantly on the horizon. A reminder not of the boy she had loved, but of her mistake.

XXVII

I drive to work but find the road blocked by wreckage. There are pieces of glass and plastic strewn across four lanes. People have abandoned their vehicles to stand on the asphalt, their hair whipping faintly in the breeze.

Even in the early morning the heat is punishing. I watch the city shimmering ahead of me, the light waves dancing as they pass through the air. The longer I sit the more I feel drowsiness settling upon me, freeing me from the burden of consequence.

I kill the engine and wait for the sound of sirens but the road is still deathly silent over half an hour later. A nervous energy begins to grip me. I think of the boy on the highway. The stationary traffic, the great mass of bodies surging forward over the hoods of cars. The scene feels so eerily familiar that I abandon any hope of making it into work and turn round, crossing the grass median to head back the way I came.

I leave the freeway and opt instead for a more scenic route. Half of the shopfronts I pass have their shutters drawn, the rest are in the process of closing. People stand in the street arguing over groceries. Children hold cardboard signs offering fair rates on bottled water and canned goods. Homeowners nail wooden boards across their windows as if preparing for an approaching storm.

I drive largely unimpeded, all of the traffic heading out over the water in the opposite direction. I can see the sun shimmering across the top of a long convoy of cars. The families I pass sit and fan themselves in the heat, their roof racks full with camping supplies and hunting equipment, the tools necessary for a new type of survival.

When I get home Simone is working in the vegetable garden. She watches me approach without emotion. I bend and kiss her forehead.

'People are uneasy in the city,' I say. 'They think it'll be here soon.'

I stand and lean against the greenhouse, fanning myself. I notice the flowers inside are all long dead, the soil cracked and broken. At the back of my eye socket I feel a migraine beginning to stir, waking itself from some dormant phase. 'My God is it hot,' I say.

Simone shifts restlessly, inspecting the palms of her hands.

'I think we've got a decision to make,' I tell her. 'We either leave with the rest of them, or we dig in here.'

'I won't leave,' she says, folding her arms defensively. 'I won't leave him.'

'We wouldn't be leaving him, we'd be leaving this place.'

'I can feel him here.'

'What does that mean?'

'It means I can feel him here.'

She sits on her knees among rows of pockmarked peppers and tomatoes. I notice for the first time that the vegetables are all slowly succumbing to blossom-end rot. I pick one up and hold it in my hand, its base sunken, its skin discoloured, and it's only then that I realise the significance. The cause of her anxiety.

Each year she would harvest the vegetables with Phineas. They would sit together in the kitchen and squeeze the pulp into Mason jars. When the juices fermented they would sieve them through and collect the seeds, ready for the next season. It was Phineas's favourite part of the entire process. He would label each jar with jagged lettering and she would keep them stacked in the pantry. The crop had been born from the last of those seeds, and now the heat was trying to take them from her.

'It will be here soon,' I tell her. 'Do you not understand?'

'Just go if you want to,' she says. 'Leave. Go on one of your drives.'

She turns her attention back to the vegetable garden. I stare at her incredulously. She seems to have resigned herself to her fate. As the rest of the country fights for its survival she instead chooses to stay and languish. She is sick, I tell myself. She is sick but she makes no effort, no attempt to get better.

'Don't do that. Don't make me out to be the villain. I'm not callous. Do you think I want any of this? Do you think I want to leave?'

'I think that's exactly what you want.'

I grit my teeth so hard that I can hear them grinding in my skull. For a moment I imagine wrapping the garden hose tightly round her neck. I imagine her fingernails raking my skin, digging into the tops of my thighs as she tries desperately to relieve the pressure round her throat. How long would she suffer, I wonder? Would she apologise in her final moments?

'I am not leaving,' she says again. 'I can feel him here. I feel his presence.'

'Well, I feel his absence. It's like a stain on this place.'

I leave her and skulk round to the side of the house. I walk along the stone path where Phineas first learnt to ride his bike. I pass beds full of plants slowly wilting in the heat, their stems hunched, their petals drooping. I turn on the spigot, kneel down and place my head beneath the freezing water. It soaks my hair and runs down the length of my back and for a moment the afternoon heat abates.

When I stand I notice the paintwork of the house is chipped and faded, bleached beneath the baking sun. I run my fingers over it and small flakes come away in my hand. I crush them in my palm and let the powder sift through my fingers.

I look at Phil's house. I see his manicured lawn, his immaculate house, and I wonder if he was born with a sort of internal GPS. A divine navigator. Something that helps him glide so casually, so effortlessly, through life.

I think of the rotting vegetables in the garden, the peeling paintwork of the house, and I feel a great pressing weight. Houses, lifestyles, relationships. Everything in need of such constant maintenance.

I consider for a moment abandoning Simone. Just taking the car and leaving. My shame radiates through me. I stare up at the sun, the sweat rolling down the length of my back, soaking a gradient into my shirt, and I feel my vision begin to tighten. I see the world around me vignetted at the edges. My vision, my entire body, funnelling downwards. The light around me growing ever dimmer.

XXVIII

I stumble up the staircase, swallowing deep panicked breaths. I feel a great rumbling beneath my feet but when I reach out to steady myself I realise that the house stands firm, that I am the one who is shaking.

I hear the sound of falling water like a drum. I clasp my hands over my ears. It thunders throughout the hallways of the house, reverberating off ceilings and windowpanes.

I know that I should phone the numbers they broadcast. That I should report my symptoms. But to what end? In the dark of my mind I see unmarked cars parked on the street, men in uniforms rushing up the driveway.

I had spent hours, entire days, begging Simone to flee the oppression of the house, the encroaching terror of the sickness. But she remains tethered to this place, to an obligation that no longer exists. She changes his bedsheets. She straightens his room. She waits by the door as if she expects him to walk through it at any moment. I know that if I leave without her, if I allow them to take me, I will never be able to return. That I will lose a part of her, of Phineas, forever.

I stumble into the bedroom and hastily check my eyes in the bathroom mirror. There is no redness, no signs of any inflammation. I call out to Simone but she does not answer. She either cannot hear me or simply chooses not to.

I strip myself naked and lie on the cool of our bed.

I think about the boy on the highway. I close my eyes and try to imagine Simone's face fading before me. I see her reduced to nothing and I feel a prickling across my skin. A chill that radiates from the base of my feet and out of the tips of my fingers.

I know that in my grief I bear some responsibility for Simone's isolation. That my emotional reticence, my inability to articulate, has at times left her feeling alone to carry the weight of our sorrow. But I feel it all. It plays on the inside of my eyelids at night. It stops my heart and I wish desperately that I could tell her all of the things I have kept from her.

Like how I once followed a small child in a shopping mall because he had blond hair like Phineas's, and he was wearing a striped shirt like the one she loved. How I had called his name and wished so badly for it to be him. But when the child turned to face me he regarded me only with confusion, and I felt such a great vacuum of affection when he took his father's hand that my legs went weak and I collapsed beside a parked car.

How in the weeks after his death when I drank I saw a dark twin in my own reflection. A callous stranger that inhabited my body in those before times. A devil who held the world in his hands but regarded it all with such a cold indifference.

In my mind I itemise my transgressions: all of the early mornings I spent wishing so badly for the boy to cease existing (wishing desperately to return to bed, for a little more sleep), all of the evenings I would return home from a hard day's work and tower over him, his eyes as keen and boundless as a golden retriever's, and I would snap at him to clean up his toys.

And perhaps worst of all, how I feel myself losing him now, the grip of my memory loosening each day. I see his face disintegrating in my mind. I forget the colour of his eyes, the sound of his laughter. I struggle to remember the shape of his face, or the smell of his hair. And I wonder when, not if, the day will come when I forget his likeness completely. When his body breaks down and he is reduced to simply a vague notion.

I sit in the dark of our bedroom and wonder if maybe it is best to forget.

XXIX

In the morning we are drawn downstairs by a commotion. I pull back the curtain to see tyre marks across the length of our lawn and an RV parked haphazardly next door. Phil and his son take turns running back and forth from the house, loading supplies. Helen stands on the porch, itemising their possessions aloud. Phil considers each for a moment before rendering a verdict, a sweaty arbiter.

'The winter coats?' she asks.

'Pack them.'

'The portable stovetop?'

'Grab it.'

'Bedding?'

'I've packed some already.'

'The photo albums?' she asks hopefully.

'Leave them.'

'Phil—' she says.

'There's no room,' he snaps back.

I dress quickly and leave the house to find Phil

packing items into the RV. Strapped to his shoulder is an old hunting rifle that I haven't seen before.

'Is everything alright over there?' I call out as I approach the edge of the property, careful not to startle him.

Helen stands motionless on the porch as if caught in the middle of some grave indiscretion. Their son Josh emerges from the darkness of the house and stands in front of her defensively.

'Everything's fine,' Phil says, turning awkwardly to position himself in front of the RV, to create a physical barrier. When he shifts his weight I catch a glimpse of the vehicle's rear compartment and realise it is packed floor to ceiling with pallets of canned goods and bottled water.

'Did you take that stuff from the store?' I ask.

'It's my store,' Phil says defensively.

'The deliveries are getting scarcer. You know that.'

I step over the threshold of the property but before my other foot can touch the ground Phil raises his rifle and levels it at my chest. 'Stay back!' he shouts. 'Helen, Josh, get in the car.'

My heart begins a strange sort of dance.

'Calm down,' I say. 'This is ridiculous.'

'I don't want to hurt you,' he says, feeling the weight of the weapon in his hands.

I study the gun as if I am looking at an alien artefact, something far from where it belongs. I regard it in the same way Phil and Helen came to regard us after the accident. To them we became displaced and destitute people. Though they offered their condolences, though Helen cooked meals and delivered them to our doorstep, they treated us with an almost superstitious aloofness. As if our sadness, our loss, was somehow infectious. We were marked by his death and they avoided us with deft hands, careful to maintain appearances but never to offer intimacy for fear that they themselves might become tainted.

'You're hoarding food. What about the rest of us? What will we do?'

'It's different for you,' he says, and casts a watchful eye towards his son. I take a long look at him. His eyes wide, his mouth contorted. I realise I have never met this man before me. He is panicked, ashamed. He is not the Phil that I once knew. He studies his son's face and I see his grip on the firearm loosen somewhat. He takes a pack of bottled water from the vehicle and throws it onto the ground between us.

'That won't last the two of us a week,' I say. 'This is ridiculous. You're abandoning your home. To go where? Where will you go?'

'As far east as we can get,' he says, slamming the RV doors shut.

I think of the East Coast. I think of all the possible roads that lead there. I think of the homes along the way. I think of a great migration of people, unsettled and disenfranchised. Driven from their homes and drawn eastward, like animals, by the gradual erosion of their natural habitat.

I see women and children and men of all ages clambering up a steep cliff face, barely navigating the rocky terrain, the ground trampled and slick beneath them. And one by one they reach the apex only to tumble down to the sea beyond. Their ruined bodies collecting in the surf, stacking up to create entirely new geographies. Mountains upon endless mountains of the sick, the dead and the dying.

I close my eyes and when they reopen I realise I've lost track of time. Phil and his family, the RV, are gone. The street is quiet. In the distance I imagine that I can see the city, alive and all-consuming. The clouds far above it churning like waves.

XXX

I sit in the dark of the study with only the television for company. The news of mass disappearances and hysteria now so frequent, so normative, that it has become an established reality. The illness so devastating that its absence would cause greater panic than its continued existence.

In cities all over the country people staple photographs of missing friends and family members to telegraph poles and noticeboards. They tie notes and trinkets to chain-link fences. They hold candlelit vigils. The bereaved trail behind vacant coffins. The bodies of their loved ones missing like the casualties of some great war.

I flip through the channels listlessly. Outside the cicadas hum and I feel my mind wandering in search of simpler times. I circle endlessly round my argument with Simone in the garden.

It's with a dull ache that I must admit to romanticising the act of disappearance. For as long as I can remember, whenever the cacophony of my life has reached an unbearable pitch, I have considered vanishing. As a child I was fascinated by ghost towns. Areas abandoned due to pollution, lawlessness, prolonged droughts. Their inhabitants fleeing so quickly in the night that they left piping hot dinners on tables and front doors ajar.

I found a calming, almost meditative bliss in the notion that a name, an entire life, could be abandoned. When I found myself dithering or unnecessarily consumed by worry I would reduce my life to a series of interpersonal connections. It became a mental exercise. How many people would have to disappear before my own existence was forgotten? Before my actions were free of consequence?

But the unfortunate truth is that the immediacy of disappearance betrays the reality of the undertaking. It must be carefully planned in order to succeed. You must squirrel money away over a long period of time. Small amounts, accrued gradually, so as not to arouse suspicion. An extra little bit from the ATM at the convenience store, cash back when paying at the till. Never any large or unexplained transactions. Nothing that could betray your true intentions. No cards, no paper trail. And you would need supplies. A bag of clothes and other essentials tucked away in the garage. A collection of road atlases and motel listings. A burner phone.

In the stillness of the study I fantasise about the breathless thrill of the act. In my mind I am never the perpetrator of such infidelities, but rather a spectator watching an alternate version of myself. A dark reflection. I imagine the hammering of my heart as I fetch my bags and throw them into the back of the car.

I sit and watch my future play out in a sort of montage.

I head west, the road before me illuminated in wide arcs. I see palm trees and tropical drinks with those little paper umbrellas. I see a barrage of motel rooms and late mornings. At some point I swap my car for an open-top convertible and use it to snake along the coastline like a shadow.

I can almost feel the sea spray. It cleanses me. I feel the breeze catching in my hair, playing with my shirt collar, and with each passing moment I seem to shed more weight, until I feel as though I can practically levitate, until I have become completely unencumbered.

I spend my days betting on horses and when either my luck runs out or the sun runs off I go in search of loose women. I fuck them behind bars and on the hoods of cars. I take them from behind, their hair wrapped tightly in my clenched fist. And when they gasp and then beg for me to slow down I thunder on, as if I am trying to rip them apart. I stop only when, at last, I am sated.

But the fantasy falls apart almost as quickly as it materialises. The logistics rendered suddenly laughable. How would I rent a convertible without providing some form of identification?

Who were these loose women, and where was this disposable income coming from?

I think again of the boy on the highway.

I sit perfectly still and try to visualise the internal mechanics of my own body. To disassemble my molecular structure. To reduce my body to its purest form. To release a lifetime of guilt and regret. Until I am left with only the goodness in me.

But I find the person who remains unrecognisable.

We would be strangers in the street.

I would pass him and he would pass me, and we would share not a single glance.

XXXI

I lift myself wearily from the chair and am preparing for bed when I spot a faint light dancing in the window of Phil and Helen's house. I switch off the television, kneel at the window and watch. The thin beam moves with a nefarious purpose. Leaping forward and stopping suddenly, lingering on various items before eventually moving on.

Had they turned back? Realised the futility in trying to outrun the sickness? Perhaps they'd been stopped at the state line, or run into some impassable congestion on the highway? But if that were the case why wouldn't they turn on their lights?

I lift the curtain back gently, so as not to attract the attention of the light, and peer round to look for the RV in the driveway but there's no sign of it.

From the garage I run barefoot in a diagonal line, avoiding the security lights at the front of the house and arriving silently at their back door. I find it locked so I circle the property, searching desperately for a way inside.

There's no evidence of any forced entry. No open

windows or doors. As far as I can tell the house is shut up tight. But through the curtains I can make out the faint shape of a person, and the beam of a flashlight sweeping from room to room.

I look back at our house and search the upstairs windows for any sign of life. I should turn back, I tell myself. But to what end? Who would I call? The emergency services are stretched past capacity. It would take them hours to respond, if they were to respond at all. And where would it end? If looting had broken out it wouldn't be long before we were targeted. Before the scenes on television were at our doorstep, taking place in our homes.

Before I'm conscious of making any sort of decision I find myself prying the mesh screen off the back door. I work quickly, bending the metal back and using a small rock to shatter a pane of glass close to the handle.

Inside the taste of stale air greets me. I sweep through the downstairs rooms as quietly as possible. I grit my teeth each time a footstep results in the creak of a floorboard, or I clumsily nudge an ornament, but I find no sign of any intruder. The lower floor of the house seems largely undisturbed.

It's only when I reach the foot of the staircase that I notice a light moving upstairs. It's yellow and casts strangely beautiful patterns across the roof, like the reflection of sunlight on water. I grip the carpet and ascend the staircase, dragging my shoulder along the curvature of the wall to steady myself. With my free hand I grope the air in front of me, feeling my way in the darkness.

At the top of the staircase I spot the figure of a woman. I call out to her. 'What are you doing here?'

She turns to face me and I realise that it's our therapist. She stands motionless in the hallway. From the centre of her chest I see the cold yellow light shimmering. I stare into it, mesmerised. I feel the edges of my vision begin to vibrate like piano wire. I feel drawn to her.

She smiles and I remember countless summer nights spent with Phineas catching fireflies in the twilight of our yard. How he would place them into plastic jars and hold them aloft like lanterns, the insects inside flashing to attract prey and partner alike. Their cold light intoxicating, their glow all-consuming.

'What are you doing here?' I ask again as the therapist turns without a word and disappears through a doorway. I follow her and watch as she opens another and steps through it. I follow her on and on, through countless doorways. The house expanding before me, twisting itself into an impossible labyrinthian structure.

I call out to her, but she does not respond.

She begins to run and I struggle to keep pace. She stops opening doors and instead begins barrelling into them, driving her shoulder into the hardwood until the frames splinter and the hinges give way. We crash through so many rooms that they become an indistinct blur.

Each time I crash through and fall into the room beyond, I find myself back in the hallway. Each time I break in, I am suddenly locked out. Until eventually I realise that I am no longer chasing our therapist at all, but myself. I see a thousand versions of my own body stretching out before me in a vanishing line, as if I have become stuck between two great mirrors.

Each time the door tears from its hinges I catch a glimpse of the room beyond. I see Simone sat in an overflowing bathtub, her face bloated as if from some horrific allergy. I cry out to her. I beg for her to let me in. I break down door after door after door. I scream for her, but know that it's hopeless. I feel alone in the way an animal must when it knows the end is near.

I drive my shoulder once again into the wood and it finally gives way with a sickening crack. The door lurches open with an air of finality, and I step through it to find myself at home once again. I stand alone in the master bathroom and strain my ears to hear in the darkness. The house is quiet.

I inspect the bathroom but find nothing out of the ordinary. I wash my face in the sink and stare at myself in the mirror. It's curious, I think to myself, that I can't recall the last time I set foot in here.

I lie down in bed beside Simone and am asleep before I'm even sure that's what I'm driving at.

In the morning she rolls over to face me.

'I dreamt we were at sea,' she says.

I contemplate telling her about my dream but think better of it. When she stands and drifts down into the belly of the house I dress and once again inspect the door to the master bathroom. I'm surprised to find a hairline fracture running the length of the frame. Fresh screws affixing the hinges.

XXXII

Days pass. The sickness draws ever closer, bringing with it an unrelenting heat. Missouri is quickly overrun and the neighbourhood comes alive with a nervous energy. Some pack their belongings and flee. I watch them leave with an impending sense of dread. Simon refuses to evacuate. I abandon all hope of convincing her and instead resolve myself to preparing for what lies ahead.

I gather up as many containers and buckets as I can find and fill each of them with water. I plug the sinks and fill them too. Though I briefly consider filling up the tub in the master bathroom, I find I can't bring myself to go anywhere near it. Instead I slip over to Phil and Helen's house and fill theirs.

I raid their cupboards for canned goods and other non-perishable foods, stuffing them in a sheet and lugging them back to our pantry where I perform a full inventory. We have enough food to last us, I don't know, a month, maybe, if we rationed carefully?

I briefly consider the immense privilege of having absolutely no idea how much food a human being consumes on a weekly basis, and then try to push the fear of watching what was once plentiful grow scarce from my mind.

I sort the perishables by their sell-by dates and try to assure myself that all of this is an academic exercise. There's no reason they'd shut off the utilities. But stranger things have happened, and if it came to it there would be no warning.

From the back porch I look towards the city. How long could modern infrastructure survive without human interaction? Were there fail-safes in place for this kind of eventuality? Could the water and electrical systems operate autonomously? If so, for how long? If the illness swept away the city's population would we feel the aftershocks immediately, or would it take time for the impact to ripple out into the suburbs?

I water the vegetable garden profusely, though it seems to have become an exercise in futility. No matter how much attention we pay to it, the crop continues to spoil. Nevertheless, I let the hose run until the ground beneath my feet is a bog.

It's then that I remember the compost bin at the foot of the garden. A freestanding plastic drum that could easily hold a few hundred gallons of water.

I tip it onto its side and scrape out the damp contents with my hands. I remove autumn leaves and dirt, but am surprised when my hand wraps round a lilac-coloured ribbon. I pull at it and from the mouth of the drum emerges a floral wreath that I don't recognise. I reach inside and find another, and then another. The drum is full of them. The flowers long dead, but still held together in their bouquets.

Attached to one is a card. I wipe the dirt from it and hold it up to the light. The writing is hard to decipher, but I can make out my name. I lay each of the bouquets on the ground, like tiny bodies, and inspect them. Every single one is tied with purple ribbon. I feel my mind searching desperately in the heat. I know that there is relevance to the discovery, but no part of it sparks recognition.

XXXIII

I sit in the shade of the garden and think of Phil and Helen and their son, Josh. I wonder where they might be at this exact moment. I see several possible futures playing out simultaneously in my mind.

In one I see their bodies strewn unnaturally about the RV, the windscreen a spiderweb of broken glass. The doors ajar and bullet-riddled. Their pallets of water and canned goods long gone.

In another I see them pulling into the parking lot of some pristine government facility. I see men in hazmat suits escorting them into medical tents. I see Josh lying nervously on his stomach as a nurse sterilises the base of his spine, and I see a tired-looking doctor injecting a serum into the bone. I see the family reunite behind the fortified walls of the compound, finally free from the burden of the illness.

I think of Phineas and how we would have handled things differently were he still here. I see the three of us leaving in Phil and Helen's RV and heading east, our families safe in greater numbers.

I see us setting up camp and learning to live off the land, far from the mess of the cities. We sleep in shifts, and at night we tell stories round the campfire, the absence of technology resurrecting the pastime of conversation.

Saprotrophic nutrition.

Wasn't that what the therapist had called it?

One existence nourished by the death of another?

But was that not the case of all acts of parenthood and creation? A series of sacrifices made so that a child may flourish. Had we not sacrificed parts of ourselves? Our lifestyle, our own relationship, so that Phineas could live?

We imbued him with our own aspirations and desires. And we did so under the selfish notion that he would carry them long into the future, long after we were gone from the earth.

We carried him so that he might one day carry us.

We grieve his death now by remembering his life. But is it the responsibility of the living to harbour the dead, or is that a similar kind of selfishness? Is he tethered by our memories of him? Forced to forever walk the chambers of our heart as some half-remembered phantom?

When I try to imagine the afterlife I see a cave surrounded by such endless outer darkness. The yellow light of our shared existence reflecting endlessly against its wet flowstone walls. The light of the dead carried from hand to fumbling hand. Until those shaking hands grow weak, until no hands remain.

I look up to see Simone rise from the porch swing and slip back into the house. I call out to her but the sound is drowned out from overhead as a convoy of military helicopters flies low over the house and heads towards the city.

XXXIV

Outside there is pandemonium in the street, the arrival of the military having ignited some incendiary spark. Stoking a fire that has raged beneath us for some time but that has now risen from cracks in the ground to lick openly at our heels.

Women carry screaming children into car seats. Fathers grapple with backpacks and other pieces of hastily packed luggage. A minivan backs blindly into the road and collides with the back of a sedan, sending both vehicles spinning out of control.

We watch as people tear up lawns and jockey for position, trying desperately to avoid the growing pile-up of cars.

It's only when an elderly couple emerge from their home and wander into the road that the commotion dies down. Their bodies are swollen, the whites of their eyes red. They hold hands and drift dreamily along the asphalt before embracing each other in a kiss.

The onlookers watch in silence as their skin turns

transparent and their bodies knit together. Their muscles and tendons merging into a purple mass before falling away, like petals, to reveal a network of nerves that intertwine and then splay out in the wind.

They rise from the ground and ascend, nerves cast behind them like the branches of a willow tree.

For a moment there is an unnatural stillness to the air, a delicate peace. Then a shot rings out, clear and clean as if heard from across the crystalline surface of a lake, and chaos resumes. The elderly woman, still cocooned in her husband's nervous system, grows opaque, her pale skin reappearing.

Inside her body a cloud of red expands, like the butterfly of an inkblot test. I see a bullet lodged deep in the cavity of her chest. As she re-materialises and falls to the ground the nerves that make up her husband's fingers reach out for her desperately. The shape of his anguished face outlined in furious red.

She lands with a dull thud and lies panting on the asphalt, taking deep laboured breaths that gradually slow, and he lifts his head skyward with a look of sad determination. Preparing for a reality he could never imagine but must now inhabit.

A second shot rings out.

This time the bullet meets a car windscreen, the sound ricocheting off the once quiet suburban landscape. People crawl on their stomachs to their cars. Others double over and take cover against the sides of houses. Children scream. People call out the names of their loved ones. Gradually the street empties.

Cars move slowly to avoid hitting the body. And though she reaches her hand up occasionally to grip at their hubcaps none of them ever consider stopping. The fact that they avoid her at all is a small mercy.

XXXV

When we phone for an ambulance the line rings but there is no answer. We fetch a portable radio from the kitchen and find it awash not with static but silence. On the television the studios are now all empty. News desks stand unattended. Traffic cameras show mile-long lines of unoccupied cars.

When the last of the neighbours depart I leave the safety of the house and stand over the woman in the street. I see her chest rising and falling in frantic bursts, her breathing short and sharp. Her head engorged by the sickness, the edges of her face mushroomed outwards. Her red eyes searching frantically for some imagined horizon.

'She's alive,' I call out to Simone. 'She's still alive. We have to help her.'

'There's nothing we can do,' she says, shuffling anxiously on the porch. 'There's nothing anyone can do.'

'We have to at least try,' I say, scooping her up in my arms.

'Where will you take her? The hospital? They can't help her. Even if they wanted to, they couldn't.'

'A clinic, then. There has to be someone left.'

'You can't fix her.'

'We can't just leave her here, Simone. I'm going to get help.' I look out at the street, towards the city. I feel it calling me. 'Come with me,' I say desperately.

She shakes her head. 'I can't. I just can't.'

I lift the woman into the back seat of the car and lay a blanket over her. I run my hand through her shock of white hair and try not to look at the ugly red blotch on her shirt. It clings uncomfortably to the skin beneath, rising and falling with each laboured breath. I place my hand over it helplessly, feeling weak.

'I'll be back soon. I promise. I'll come back for you,' I say.

Simone bows her head. I put the car in reverse and back out of the driveway. I don't need to look for her in the rear-view mirror to know what I'll see.

XXXVI

We slalom through the traffic and make our way into the city. We pass several vehicles heading in the opposite direction. They flash their lights and sound their horns to warn us of what lies ahead.

The act of disappearance seems to have happened more quickly in the city. We see the outbound traffic gradually begin to wane until the cars we pass are all empty, silent except for their idling engines. Some have managed to pull to the shoulder before succumbing to the sickness. Others have vanished at breakneck speeds, sending their vehicles into the backs of others.

On the outskirts of the city the buildings creak and groan. The wind whips loose paper and trash high into the air. I see fires raging on the horizon. Smoke pillars that rise to hold up the sky. I see ash falling like snow against the windshield.

I stop the car multiple times to clear away debris. When I get back behind the wheel I hold up my hands and find that they are black with soot.

On the highway we pass the smoking remnants of a news helicopter.

'It's the end of the world,' I say.

The white-haired woman writhes on the back seat.

'Jennifer?' she calls out. 'Jennifer?'

I tell her no and she mumbles incoherently.

XXXVII

It's obvious that the hospital is deserted before I even kill the engine but I park up anyway and tell the woman I'll be back with help. She speaks in frantic whispers, reaching out with her hands to cup some imagined face. When I step out of the car the heat of the late afternoon hits me and I think better of leaving her alone. I swaddle her in a blanket and scoop her into my arms.

Outside the sky is the colour of bruised skin – the sun setting slowly over a skyline now thick with smoke – and I feel a sudden urgency to my work, as if the falling darkness will swallow all that it touches.

I call out for help in corridors and waiting rooms but find no response. With each footstep I feel myself becoming the sound of my own voice. Desperate, frantic. Searching for something that cannot be found.

I walk through wards full of machinery and empty beds. The floors wet with leaking IV lines. The air saturated by the shrill calls of dialysis machines and heart monitors. They speak in a foreign dialect. The language of grief not universal at all, but individualistic, coded. Woven into the fabric of people in a way that makes it impossible to fully decipher.

'I'm tired,' she says, wrapping her arm round my neck and drawing herself into me in the way a child might.

She is impossibly light in my arms. I imagine that she could be Phineas, and when I close my eyes I see his crooked smile floating in the dark of my mind like some disembodied phantom.

I lay the woman down on a gurney. Her breathing shallow. Her head engorged. She takes my face in her hands.

'My husband?' she asks, and I shake my head. I don't know where he is, or even what he is any more.

'Is there anyone you'd like me to call?' I ask, and the woman shakes her head.

'What about Jennifer? You asked for her in the car?'

'My sister,' she says. 'She's gone.'

'One of the disappeared?'

She shakes her head no. 'We were young when it happened.'

I fetch her a glass of water and sit beside her in one of those uncomfortable plastic chairs that seem to plague classrooms and hospitals. Across the ward, on a shelf by the window, is an antique anatomical bust of the male body. Some of the organs have been removed and arranged round the figurine like offerings.

I think back to my conversation with the therapist. To the belief that we parcel ourselves up and give parts of ourselves away. That the body is a house occupied by those whom we love and have loved. But the same was true for those we have hurt, those we have failed. We harbour their pain and we pass it on. We inflict it catastrophically and infinitesimally. Piecemeal and in perpetuity.

The silence between us grows lustful, wanting. The woman winces and adjusts herself on the gurney. 'I saw her today, when it happened.'

'What was it like?' I ask.

She's quiet for a long time. 'It felt easy.'

I feel an imagined and distant rumbling, as if the earth is yawning, waiting playfully to swallow me whole. 'There is someone I would desperately like to see again,' I say, rubbing circles into my palms.

'They won't be the way you remember them, not exactly. They are changed. Imagine everyone you have ever met, even in passing. Lovers, guardians, mentors, strangers in the street. Imagine every word you have ever spoken to another living soul. Then imagine yourself as a composite of those remembrances.'

It feels as though a knot has been tied at the centre of my head. A thousand hands reach out of the darkness to pull it tight.

'I don't understand,' I say.

'We don't fall in love with people, but rather versions of people. Manifestations. The act of love renders them incorporeal. We carry the idea of a person even as their reality ages and dies before us.'

The woman winces again, holding her stomach, sucking in breath.

'We never truly stop falling in love because the act of living is itself a process of constant reincarnation, a perpetual reconciliation between what was once and what is now.'

'But there is danger in it,' I say. 'The risk that reality diverges too harshly from expectation, from desire.'

'You're beginning to see,' says the woman, and I notice that the room has filled with a cold yellow light. It bounces off the ceiling and pools on the floor, like sunlight on water. I've seen this before, I think to myself, and turn to see our therapist standing in the hallway.

'It's time for you to go,' the woman says.

I stare at the therapist.

'I can't just leave you here,' I say to the woman.

'I'm not staying, dear. It's time for me to go too. We're just headed in separate directions.'

XXXVIII

The therapist wanders lazily out of the hospital and I follow behind her. I feel a swirling beneath my navel. A mixture of arousal and fear. She steps into the street without so much as a glance and I call out to warn her but of course it's deserted. It will remain so for a long time, likely until the wilderness reclaims it.

She slips into the back seat of my car and I get behind the wheel. I look at her in the rear-view mirror. 'What do you want?' I ask.

'I want you to drive,' she says, picking at one of her cuticles. So I drive. We are alone in the world now. I wind the window down and hear nothing but the steady thump of rubber on asphalt.

'Is there anything more terrifying than the absence of sound?' I ask.

'Is there anything sadder than spending your days longing for it?' she responds.

In the back seat I watch her recline.

'Am I sick? Is any of this real?' I ask.

She sighs heavily, leaning her head back to stare at the sky through the rear window. 'All of this time and you're still asking the wrong questions.'

'I don't understand what you want.'

'Let's try a memory exercise,' she says, clapping her hands together in frustration. 'What's the first thing you can remember about the day Phineas died?'

Outside I can see the last rays of sunlight filtering through the treetops and am surprised to find that we are no longer on the highway at all but a winding mountain road bordered by pine trees on both sides.

I search my mind desperately. 'I don't know. I got up with him. We made breakfast. Simone slept in. She'd been away at a conference and got in late.'

'That's good. What else?'

The act of remembering is physically exhausting, like working an atrophied muscle. I feel the sting of memory. 'When Simone got up she suggested we go to the beach, since we hadn't seen much of each other lately.'

'You're paraphrasing.'

'This is pointless.'

'I want to hear you say the words,' she says.

The memory is distant. I pull it through the pink of my mind and it sinks in, like dental floss against gums. The taste of iron fills my mouth. 'She said she dreamt we were at sea. She wanted to spend the day by the water.'

Outside the trees grow immeasurably tall, their

tips reaching as if to pierce the sky. The sides of the road now walled off completely by endless woodland. There are no road signs, no houses. No parked cars. Everything we pass is swallowed by darkness. I see the world a few feet at a time, illuminated by my headlights.

'Who does this help, this endless repetition?' I ask the therapist.

'Close your eyes,' she says. 'Tell me something good.'

I think of the first time I kissed Simone. How my stomach cramped and the room simmered and my heart beat so heavily it felt like my body was oscillating. And what was it I said? 'So that's what lips are for?' And how she laughed. But it felt revelatory.

And though I haven't spoken aloud the therapist says, 'Tell me how the two of you met.'

'We met through work. Separate companies, but our offices were in the same building. We ran into each other from time to time at lunch. She'd tie her hair up with these beautiful ribbons. I thought it was cute. I'd watch from my office window for a woman with ribbon in her hair.'

I have had my eyes shut for what feels like minutes. When I open them I find that I am no longer driving, but being driven. The car barrelling forward, snaking round the bends of the mountain path of its own accord.

'Did you blame her for his death?'

'A part of me did. A part of me hated her. But I could see that she blamed herself more than I ever could, more than I had any right to. It was a hot day. She was exhausted. She closed her eyes for a second.'

'Did you argue about it?'

'About culpability? No. We actively avoided discussing it. It simply became "the accident". But her feelings were clear. To her it was indefensible.'

'But that wasn't entirely the case, was it?' the therapist asks.

I grip the steering wheel until my knuckles turn white. In the dark of my mind I feel brief bursts of light. I remember shaking her awake on the beach towel. I remember the ambulance arriving and pronouncing him dead. I remember the police taking statements at the hospital.

But more than anything I remember waiting desperately for her to ask me where I'd been. Why I'd wandered off and left them both there. Because I could see that she was tired. It haunted me. In the darkness of our bedroom I would lie next to her and try to build the courage to admit that I'd wandered off because I needed a break. She'd been away all week at that stupid conference, and I wanted desperately to spend the day at home. To be rid of him. To be alone with myself. But the longer I remained silent the greater the injustice became, the more apparent my selfishness.

'When Simone told me she was pregnant I remember thinking: this is it. It was time to rise to the occasion. To become the man she deserved. But I stayed the same and she grew. Throughout the pregnancy she'd chart her progress in the bathroom mirror. I'd brush my teeth and she'd say, "Today he's the size of a sesame seed." Then a blueberry, and a few weeks later a grape. She bought him clothes and furnished his room. She stocked talc powder and baby wipes in preparation. "He's the size of an aubergine," she'd say, and hand me cases of nappy rash ointment.'

I put my foot on the brake but the car fails to stop. I take my hands from the wheel entirely and find it turns on its own. We continue to skulk up the steep incline of the mountain. I feel the pull of gravity in my stomach.

'I came home from work one day and her feet had swollen so badly she looked like a cartoon. She told me he was the size of a honeydew melon and that he had a favourite song. I didn't believe it until she put it on the stereo and let me feel him bouncing around in there.'

I sob openly, resting my head against the driver's side window. Searching desperately in the wing mirrors for any sign of flashing lights. A routine traffic stop. An authority figure.

'She carried him for nine months. He grew inside her. What did I do, besides paint his room a pea green and put together a couple pieces of flatpack furniture? She gave herself to him. She became his home. Can you imagine anything so intimate?'

When it was time I drove her to the hospital in the dead of night. She panted in the passenger seat, clutching her belly. I told her hold on, just hold on. Sometimes at night I close my eyes and I can still see the streetlights swaying in the storm winds. The car a life raft in the darkness.

'We got him home and everyone who came by the house said he was beautiful but I couldn't see it. It felt like a conspiracy. He was this pink, ruined thing. He ate with his eyes screwed shut. He slept that way too. And in the night when he woke and called out he looked just the same. We gave him everything we had but it still wasn't enough. I felt suffocated. I felt broken. But not Simone. At some point we switched roles. When it became too much she took the wheel. She told me hold on, just hold on. She knew that it would come right, and it did. Being his father was the great privilege of my life. But it remained difficult. Perhaps more difficult than it should ever have to be.'

I'm quiet for a moment.

'Every time I saw myself in him it made me want to run. You know how kids put their hands to glass and smear it? That's how it felt. He was this beautiful, pure thing. And my fingerprints stained him. It was like looking into a black mirror.'

XXXIX

The therapist sits up in the back seat and stares at me through the rear-view mirror. Her eyes like pools of moonlight in the dark. 'Tell me about the night you left,' she says.

I strain my eyes, trying to spot anything on the horizon that I recognise. 'This isn't where I'm supposed to be. I want to go home. It's late. Simone will be going out of her mind.'

'You're going exactly the right way. We have nothing but time. Tell me about the night you left.'

'We'd been arguing, if you could call it that.'

'What would you call it?' she asks.

'I don't know. An argument requires two parties. After the accident she just receded from her life, from our life together. She disappeared into herself. I supported her for as long as I could. I fed her, I bathed her. I begged her to dress herself, to leave the house. But every day was a constant battle. It was exhausting. I felt she'd been given adequate time to grieve. I felt I was due my turn. The chance to be selfish. To fall apart.'

'To re-become yourself?'

To re-become myself? Was that what I wanted?

My entire existence feels heavy, as though someone has been stitching weights into the muscles and tendons of my body. I feel myself treading water. I feel it rising. But I no longer fight to reach the surface. Instead I let gravity do its grisly work. Dragging me into the deep.

Down, down.

Into the black water, where light cannot go.

I sweep my feet round like a child as I search for a bottom in the way Phineas must have at the end.

'I packed a bag. I'd been stashing money away almost subconsciously. I told her I needed space. I turned my phone off and just went. I hoped that by leaving I would shock her.'

'Shock her?'

'Into caring. Back into her body. Something.'

I catch a pathetic glimpse of myself in the rear-view mirror. My eyes red from the salt of my tears. 'God forgive me.'

'So you left.'

'I drove west. I had this sad romantic notion that if I could just keep moving I'd wind up where I needed to be. That I'd discover something. Some missing or long-forgotten part of myself.'

The therapist leans her head back and laughs. 'This is my favourite part. Tell me about the women.'

I see them simultaneously. Hundreds of bodies spread out on an endless mattress, their limbs woven together, their eyes hungry, their fingers interlocked, their toes curled. I see brunettes and redheads. Blondes with shaved heads. I see tattoos and piercings. Their bodies slick and wet and writhing like sea surf. I see myself naked in the doorway and I watch as I wade into them, disappearing beneath the swell of their bodies. The tide swallowing me. Carrying me out to sea to be alone among my imagined conquests.

I see myself driving along the coast. The sea spray lapping at my skin. The air light in my lungs. I feel lifted with each stolen breath. Until the car leaves the road altogether. Until I am levitating above the curvature of the earth. Weightless, unencumbered. Flung like a comet out of the atmosphere to drift eternally along the firmament.

'Now I want the truth,' she says.

The truth was that I never even made it out of the state. I drove until I was tired and took up residence in one of those sad highway motels with a shared communal pool. I ate takeout alone on a lumpy mattress and at night I sat by the pool and drank.

I was furious at what I perceived as Simone's weakness. Her refusal to acknowledge the reality of our situation. It surprised me how much value I placed in her ability to persevere, in her strength. How attractive I found it, and how disgusted I'd been by its disappearance. How furious it made me. I hated Phineas for what he had reduced her to.

'You once asked me what made a person a person,' I say. 'Simone refused to eat. She lost so much weight she was barely there at all. She said he had carried her heart away. That closing her eyes was the only way she could see him again. In dreams.'

The car stalks forward like a predatory animal and I am more alone than I have ever been. I think of the missing, the unending disappeared, their bodies broken down to the bare extremity of existence. The machinery of sense and memory.

XL

We climb the mountain but the mountain does not end. The cape of night hangs over us, but there are no stars. They are elsewhere tonight.

'I can't do this,' I say.

There isn't an ounce of energy left in my body. I feel as though my feet are sinking through the floor.

'You're free to leave at any time,' the therapist says and she looks briefly surprised when I open the driver's side door and roll myself out of the car, landing on the asphalt and pulling myself up weakly.

I watch the headlights of the car disappear into the darkness and for a moment I enjoy the silence. I imagine the therapist sitting calmly in the back seat as the car teeters over the edge of the mountain and then plummets, crashing to the ground and erupting in a plume of smoke and fire. But then the headlights catch me from behind, illuminating the silhouette of my body, and the car pulls up beside me once again.

'You of all people should know it's possible to leave without truly leaving,' the therapist says as

I slide back into the driver's seat. The car pushes forward again undeterred, casting us into darkness.

'What do you want from me?' I ask.

'I want you to tell me why you decided to go home,' she says.

'I missed Simone,' I say. 'I didn't want to be without her.'

That's the partial truth.

The reality is that I knew I could exist without her.

But as what?

As whom?

'So you went home? You made reparations?'

'Yes,' I say. We took it a day at a time. We agreed to visit a therapist.

'It's a nice story,' the therapist says. 'But it's not the truth.'

I begin to feel as though I've fallen down a staircase in my mind. I see the bouquets dug out of the compost bin, laid out in a neat row at the foot of the garden. Each bound by beautiful lilac ribbon – the way she kept her hair.

'You heard running water,' she says. 'When you got home you thought a pipe had burst. It was coming from the hall landing.'

I hear the plumber's voice ring out in my mind. *You had a leak here at one point.*

I close my eyes and find myself at the foot of the stairs. I climb forever, treading water. The carpets sodden. The wallpaper pockmarked and peeling from water damage. I follow the sound of running water to the master bathroom. It spills out from beneath the crack of the door.

How long had it been running?

'I called out to her but she wouldn't answer,' I say. 'So I started hammering on the door. Begging. Pleading. *Please, Simone. Please, no.*'

I drove my shoulder into the door repeatedly. Over and over and over again. I can still hear the sound of my footsteps falling heavy against the hardwood flooring like distant thunder. Until finally it came loose with a sickening crack.

I think of the hairline fracture in the doorway of the master bathroom.

The fresh screws affixing the hinges.

'I found her in the bathtub,' I weep, swallowing panicked breaths. 'They said she must have been there for days.'

Her head bloated as if from some horrific allergy.

The whites of her eyes shot red and inflamed beneath the water.

At the coroner's inquest they reconstructed her final hours with a precision that felt slanderous, the pathologist reducing her life to a series of line items. She left no note. No explanation. But her purpose seemed self-evident. She had drawn a bath and taken pills. She had waited patiently for them to take her away, for her body to slip beneath the surface of the water so that she could finally be with him. It was only when the dosage proved ineffective that she made a deep incision along her inner thigh. A violent act. One final, misguided punishment.

I remember being surprised by how clear the water

had been when I found her. My horror when I looked closer and realised that parts of her had settled at the bottom of the bathtub as a sort of black sediment. It was the darkest colour I had ever seen. Not a colour at all but rather a total absence of light.

They were both there now, beneath the black water. She had gone to find him. Her arms outstretched. Her fingers straining to hold him one last time.

I remember the ambulance arriving in the street.

I remember men in uniforms storming up the driveway.

I remember them carrying her out in a bag.

And that night in my dreams I remember standing at the edge of a lake. The water black, but unbroken. Reflective as if made out of polished glass. A perfect mirror.

From the shoreline I watched as birds dove from trees and careened along, their wingtips mere inches from the surface. I felt a great anxiety watching them, as if piercing the water would somehow amount to a terrible disaster. A great flood, perhaps. Or a famine. Something biblical.

So I resolved to sit at the water's edge like a guardian, to ward off any evildoers. To dance and shout and holler when any such attempt was made. But as I waited I felt myself drawn closer and closer to the edge. Until I was close enough to crane my neck and see my own reflection.

But when I looked I saw that I was changed.

No longer a man at all but a blanket of the same crystalline water. And upon seeing myself I wept, my tears rippling out across the surface of the water. Across the surface of my own body.

XLI

The car crests the top of the mountain road and I realise the tree line has disappeared. That it is late afternoon and we are sitting on the road outside the house.

'Is any of this real?' I whisper.

The therapist leans forward and kisses my neck gently. 'Only the parts you wish weren't,' she says.

'I don't know who I am without them,' I say.

She runs a gentle hand through my hair and I close my eyes. She leans in close and whispers, 'You are everything they knew you were, everything they hoped you could be. And you are everything they wished you weren't.'

'They were better than me.'

'Then you must be better for them.'

'Where do I go from here?' I ask.

The therapist points to the front door of the house, which opens softly to reveal a cold yellow light. 'It's time to say goodbye,' she says.

XLII

I find Simone upstairs drawing a bath. I take her hand and turn her in to me. Her pale face red from a day in the sun, her hair bound by lilac ribbon. She smiles at the sight of me and I cup her face in my hands.

I feel a tugging at my waist and lift Phineas into my arms. I kiss his alabaster cheeks, dotted by a constellation of freckles, and brush away the loose sand that seems to have worked its way into every crevice of his body.

He rests his weary head on my shoulder and I resist the urge to draw him into me, to absorb his entire being. Instead I place him into the water and kneel at the side of the tub to wash away the detritus of the day.

I wash his hair, working the shampoo into a thick lather that I press against his chin to create a comical beard. He shrieks with laughter and the sound makes me weak.

I towel him dry and Simone disappears downstairs to prepare a meal. He chooses a story and we lie together on the bed as I regale him with tales of giants and golden geese. Faraway lands.

When I hear him breathing softly against me I bury my nose into his hair and breathe him in. It is like food for the hungry. I hold him and imagine the man he could have become, and for the first time I mourn not for him, but for the world. For its collective loss.

Downstairs Simone hands me a glass of wine and we sit and eat dinner on the porch swing. After the dishes are finished she lays her feet on my lap and rests herself against a cushion. A faint breeze whips at the tops of the trees, taking the edge off the heat. I look at the vegetable garden, bursting with life, and see a similar vibrancy in Simone.

We sit together and watch the sunset. In the half-light I can hear the calls of distant animals. They speak in languages I don't recognise or perhaps simply don't care enough to understand. I know then that I must leave, that I cannot stay. Everything has its place, and this isn't mine. Not any longer.

I lead Simone into the dark of our bedroom. She lays herself down and I watch her sheer dress as it clings to her body. The effect is maddening. She removes it and for a moment I see the bodies of my imagined conquests in the space behind her. A surging mass of arms and legs, lips and thighs.

I watch as they slowly merge together to form the body of my wife.

She calls to me then, the sum of my want. And I go to her.

XLIII

In the morning I wake alone from a dream that the three of us were at sea. We worked on our hands and knees to build a shining tower that rose for miles and reflected the water all around it. A shimmering monument that grew smaller in my rear-view mirror with each passing mile.

Never vanishing completely.

Acknowledgements

Untold thanks to my wife for reading draft after draft and believing in me on the many days I couldn't bear to. She carries my heart.

Thanks to Toby and Seth, my children, who are the best of me. To my mother for her unwavering love and support. To the countless professionals working to illuminate the fields of neuroscience and psychology.

Finally, my sincere thanks to the entire team at Fairlight Books for taking such incredibly good care of me.

Bookclub and writers' circle notes for the
Fairlight Moderns can be found at
www.fairlightmoderns.com

Share your thoughts about the
book with #TherapistNovella

Also in the Fairlight Moderns series

Bottled Goods by Sophie van Llewyn

Travelling in the Dark by Emma Timpany

The Driveway Has Two Sides by Sara Marchant

Inside the Bone Box by Anthony Ferner

There Are Things I Know by Karen B. Golightly

Minutes from the Miracle City by Omar Sabbagh

Atlantic Winds by William Prendiville

Milton in Purgatory by Edward Vass

The Nail House by Gregory Baines

SOPHIE VAN LLEWYN

Bottled Goods

*Longlisted for **The Women's Prize for Fiction** 2019,
The Republic of Consciousness Prize 2019 and
The People's Book Prize 2018*

When Alina's brother-in-law defects to the West,
she and her husband become persons of interest to
the secret services and both of their careers come
grinding to a halt.

As the strain takes its toll on their marriage,
Alina turns to her aunt for help – the wife of a
communist leader and a secret practitioner of the
old folk ways.

Set in 1970s communist Romania, this novella-
in-flash draws upon magic realism to weave a
captivating tale of everyday troubles.

*'It is a story to savour, to smile at, to
rage against and to weep over.'*
—Zoe Gilbert, author of *FOLK*

*'Sophie van Llewyn has brought light
into an era which cast a long shadow.'*
—Joanna Campbell, author of
Tying Down the Lion